The
BEN-ADON
SCROLLS

To Pastor Dave
God Bless You

w E A

2 Chr 7:14

William E. Planck

ISBN 978-1-64416-115-9 (paperback)
ISBN 978-1-64416-117-3 (hardcover)
ISBN 978-1-64416-116-6 (digital)

Christian Faith Publishing, Inc.
832 Park Avenue
Meadville, PA 16335
www.christianfaithpublishing.com

Printed in the United States of America

CONTENTS

PREFACE

To the best of my knowledge, Awnee Ben-Adon and his scrolls do not exist. They are pure fiction. They are products of my imagination, but the nagging question remains, "What if?"

What if a Pharisee, during the ministry of Christ, had access to the products of, or was a part of, an intelligence gathering organization charged with gathering all the information available about any and everything that could affect their organization? And *what if* that information, which has to do with the ministry of Christ, was recorded for posterity? What form would it take, and what effect would it have on the people that were exposed to it?

All the scroll information gathered in the *Ben-Adon Scrolls* come from the writings of Matthew, Mark, Luke, John, and Acts, as recorded in a Greek version of the New Testament. Old Testament references come from a version of a Hebrew text. If some of the grammar and phraseology is strange to you, I suggest you refer your questions to my Greek and Hebrew sources.

I have attempted to keep my story in proper chronological order. If something is out of place, it is not by design. Remember, some scrolls would have a much longer travel time than others, which could upset the chronological order.

The same is true with the geographical locations and the lifestyles described. I have done my best to do them justice.

I have done my best to keep from violating the archaeological discipline of the area.

Beth Eden is a fictional location, although I am satisfied that such a place as Beth Eden did exist in one form or another at that time. Further, I am satisfied that the events recorded as taking place in Beth Eden are traditionally fitting for that place and time.

Concerning some of the terms used, "traditional" indicates that the facts given fit the time and the place but are not necessarily true. "Historical" indicates that the facts given are true to the best of my knowledge.

Some of the characters in my writings are also the products of my imagination. Others are some of the nameless characters from the writings of Matthew, Mark, Luke, and/or John that I have given names to. I have also tried to identify, as many as possible, the historical persons that played a part in the Passion. I trust I have treated them all well and justly. All the characters are listed in the "Scroll of Characters," which is found in the back of the book.

A note on pronoun capitalization: The present-day standard is to capitalize *he* and *him* when it refers to Jesus. That was not the case during the time of the ministries of John the Baptist and Jesus of Nazareth, and it is not the case in this writing. I have tried to keep my writing as time sensitive as possible. No disrespect is intended or should be inferred.

A note on unfamiliar terms, terms identified with a "*" are defined in the "Scroll of Terms" in the back of the book.

Seeing as you are one of the few who will undertake the exploration of this labor of love, I hope you will find it thought-provoking, entertaining, and something other than a waste of your time

William E. Planck

The Retreat

Two Pharisees sat at a table in a courtyard of a house in the southwest section of Jerusalem, known as the Upper City. They were facing north, and they could just begin to make out the Little and Great Bear constellations. Between them was the constellation Draco, that old serpent cast down from heaven.

As they enjoyed the cool of the evening, they were discussing some of the finer points of the Oral Law and the events of the day. Several servant girls came out of the house with fresh-baked bread, platters of dried fish and cheese, a bowl of olives, and another of figs and dates, along with a pitcher of wine, cut four to one*, and mixed with honey. They placed the items on the table, and one of them cut the cheese. After the wine was poured, the girls were dismissed by a wave of the hand from the host, Jonathan Ben-Gorion*.

The men then stood and performed the ritual washing of their hands, each pouring water for the other. Jonathan, as host, pulled his prayer shawl up over his head and offered the ritual of washing of the hands: "Blessed are you, the High Holy One of Israel, King of the universe, who has sanctified us with his commandments and commanded us concerning washing of hands."

Jonathan then offered a prayer for the food and wine: "Blessed are You, High Holy One of Israel, King of the universe, who creates varieties of nourishment, who creates the fruit of the vine, the trees,

7

and the ground. Blessed are you, through whose word everything comes into being. In the name of the Holy One of Israel, blessed is he."

The men then sat themselves, and Jonathan honored Ben-Gamaliel by gesturing to him to take the first piece of food and a cup of wine.

Shimon Ben-Gamaliel thanked his host for his prayers and helped himself to some bread, fish, and cheese. Jonathan then took some bread a bit of fish and a fig.

Gamaliel commented that it was a lovely evening.

Gorion replied that it was and then said that he wondered if Berossus* knew what he started when he invented astrology.

"Berossus didn't invent astrology. He just organized it and gave it a fancy name. People have been using the stars to make predictions of the future since pre-flood times."

Gamaliel continued their conversation by changing the subject. "The Council of Ruling Elders* has expressed a concern over news coming up from the valley. It seems that there is a new self-proclaimed prophet preaching the repentance of sins and baptizing converts near Jericho. Our people down there have taken some interest in him, and some have even gone down to be baptized. There is even talk amongst the Council of Fourteen* of sending a committee down to question him."

"A working Sadducees* outside the city? That would be something to see," Jonathan replied.

"I doubt that one of the Sadducees will go." Gamaliel continued. "They will probably send a small delegation of Levites* down. Anyway, the Council of Ruling Elders has made some special arrangements to cover this situation. Our people down there have been instructed to seek out this prophet and then do nothing more than observe and report for the time being. They are going to be sending us written reports on all that they see and hear. Some of the reports may be in Aramaic or even Greek. The Council wants them translated into classic Hebrew before they received them. Also, some of the couriers may be undesirables or even Gentiles. So they have arranged for an outsider, a mediator*, to receive them and translate the scrolls as needed. Then one of our people will pick up the reports and turn them over to the council."

Jonathan then asked, "Is everyone on the council in agreement with this?

"No. Rhodocus Ben-Merari and his followers are in objection. The plan did not originate with them, so they are politically against it."

"Has Ben-Merari always been so disagreeable? He seems to feed on being negative."

"Yes, he is his father's son, and his father taught him well. I remember when his father died, there was more delight than there were regrets."

"So who gets that job?"

"The council has selected you to do it, my friend."

"There is a man, a mediator and a writer and translator of contracts that has set up his presence just inside the door of Beth Eden*, just north and west of the Antonia*."

"I know the place. It is a Roman house of pleasure and a Gentile place of refuge."

Gamaliel nodded and continued, "This mediator is our go-between with the Romans. He has a good command of languages. His Greek name is Nicholaus. His father was a very successful Greek trader, and his mother was one of his father's Hebrew slaves. One of my students knew of him in Tarsus of Cilicia. There he was known in the Hebrew community as Awnee Ben-Adon. The council has asked that you make contact with this Nicholaus and act as the council's go-between. He in turn has been instructed to pay the couriers five silver denarii for each scroll he receives. He will be reimbursed by you from council funds and paid an additional silver denarius per scroll for his services. Here is a pouch of one hundred denarii to start the project. You are to make a weekly visit, and you will be reimbursed and paid for your services by the council each week. Make sure you retrieve the original along with his copies of each scroll. Pay him at the normal going rate for translations. You may also want to talk to him about the contents of the scrolls. He has insights that are not ours, and they may be of interest to the council."

Jonathan pondered the assignment for a few seconds. "I really don't think I even want to be seen with this mediator. I know of this 'lowly son of his master.' He breaks the Sabbath. He associates with sinners, and even writes contracts for Romans and other Gentiles. Are you sure there isn't someone else you can give this assignment to?"

"No, the assignment is yours. You are active enough to not cause too much attention by going to Beth Eden. You have found favor with the council. This assignment is of prime importance to your future. Besides, don't be so hard on the man, my friend. I have used his services in my dealings with the Romans, and he has never disappointed me. He is a Neeman*. His contracts have always stood both the test of our Law and a good close Roman examination. They have always been honored by nearly all the parties concerned. He is no anarchist. However, he does not practice political correctness, and he is no respecter of persons. He treats everyone as equals, to the chagrin of some of our members. He writes contracts on the Sabbath, true, but this is only when his clients need them on the Sabbath. He never turned anyone away, not even sinners or the poor who cannot pay. The man serves all the people, and I can't find much fault in him for that."

"Why is the council interested in the insights of this Greek outsider?"

"The man is well educated as a Greek, and he studies the Torah and writings from both Hebrew and Greek scrolls, which he purchased in Alexandria. He is a man of means and is well traveled. At one time, there was even some interest in recruiting him into our movement, but he turned us down. The man is not a good keeper of the law, true, but he is a willing tool of the council. He knows his scriptures and the Written Law. His insights will be interesting. Take the scrolls to the secretary of the council in the council chambers, and he will reimburse you and pay you your due."

"Of course, I will do as the council desires, but I still don't like the idea of having to go to Beth Eden and meet with a Greek."

"Don't worry. It won't rub off on you."

Both men laughed and continued enjoying their food, their conversation, and the cool of the evening.

Gabbai

There was a public building, larger than any other in the area, save the temple and the Antonia Fortress. It was in the commercial area, on the main road, a little north and west of the Antonia. There were no signs or marking to identify this Jerusalem paradox, but it was known to one and all as Beth Eden.

The building was a conglomerate of an evolution of connected buildings that were, for the most, three stories tall. It entertained some form of business, accommodations, and/or pleasure for just about everyone.

The first floor had two main connected buildings. Just inside the north entrance was a large public gathering area. Its primary use by the owners was for the renting of tables and the serving of food and drink. The public area was a facility for mediators and the brokers of commodities and for the bartering of goods. The owner also rents security storage rooms for those who have need of them on the west end of the main building. There was a large kitchen and pantry building to the south of the public area.

There was another long narrow connected one-story building known as the Roman Room, east of the main entrance, running north and south. It was the gathering place, and a retreat, for eating, drinking, and gaming. In the evening, Caesarea Dancing Girls entertained there.

The second floor was over the public area and was primarily a lodging area that catered to the needs of travelers. There were sleeping rooms, a public meeting, and a dining area—which featured a Gentile menu and its own kitchen—over the first-floor kitchen. There were also laundering and money-changing services available.

The third floor was a second lodging area, reserved for Mistress Abishag and her ladies with painted faces and plated hair. It also had services that catered to the special needs of their clientele.

There was one other resident, worthy of mention at this time, and that is Lady, the street dog. Generally speaking, dogs were not very popular in Jerusalem. Calling a person a dog was an insult. Lady came wandering in one day and curled up behind Ben Adon's chair. She became his constant companion and the delight of most of the residents ever since. She would go up to the second floor at mealtime, and the kitchen help always had a dish for her. The ladies of the third floor delighted in giving her a bath, grooming her, and anointing her with their sweet-smelling ointments.

*****

Jada Ben-Lahad, the jeweler, was seated at the table of Levi with a withered hand, the apprentice of Nicholaus. They were discussing a contract that Ben-Lahad needs. The contract was really an excuse for two old friends to spend some time together. Nicholaus knew this, but he didn't mind.

Eglah, Beth Eden's third-floor chore girl, came rushing up to Nicholaus's table. "Master Nicholaus, there is a man outside with a scroll. He says he must see you right away and that I must bring you out to him!"

Lady jumped up to greet Eglah, and Levi looked up with a smile on his face. Ben-Lahad had completed his visit and excused himself.

Nicholaus looked up in wonderment from his work and studied the girl for a moment. Then he said, "Tell me about this man, Eglah."

By now, Eglah had caught her breath. "He is very rude and demanding. He acts like he is a king or something. He is short and fat, and he stinks of the road. He is dressed like he comes from Jericho."

"Sit down and rest yourself, Eglah," Nicholaus said. "I need to speak to Master Levi for a moment."

Lady placed her head on Eglah's lap. Eglah calmed herself by stroking Lady's head and scratching behind her ears. Eglah then bent over for a doggie kiss.

Nicholaus thought for a few seconds. Then he turned to Levi; his table was the next one over. "Levi, Eglah will bring in a courier with a scroll. I want you to receive this courier in my name. I am going into the Roman Room, so tell him that I had been called away by the Romans. Make sure he sees your withered hand the first thing. Examine the scroll closely, and ask all the questions you can think of. Use whichever language he addresses you in. Let him see you taking notes in classic Hebrew. Do all this before you pay him. Pay him no more than five silver denarii. Offer him food and drink, but most importantly, keep him here as long as you can. When he leaves, come and get me in the Roman Room."

Levi indicated that he understood.

Nicholaus then turned to Eglah and told her, "Take your time. But go tell the man that I cannot come out to him. He must come inside to my table to see me."

"But, Master Nicholaus, what if the man won't come?"

"Oh, he will come in all right. He wants his money for the scroll. Come, Eglah, it's time to go get your man." Then Nicholaus gave Eglah ten brass dupondii and sent her on her way.

Nicholaus took up his staff and departed for the Roman Room with Lady trailing behind.

A while later, Eglah made her appearance with a stranger at her side. She had a smile on her face when she brought him to Levi's table.

"I am Gabbai of the tribe of Benjamin. Are you Nicholaus?" the stranger barked demandingly.

Meanwhile, Eglah timidly beat a hasty retreat and disappeared into the stairwell.

"No, Master. I am Levi. Nicholaus is my master."

"I must see the mediator Nicholaus," Gabbai growled.

"I'm sorry, sir, but my master was called away. He is in the next room with the Romans, if you care to join him. Or you're welcome to wait here, if you wish, until he returns. Or possibly I can help you."

"My master was in a hurry to get this scroll up here and to get his money. Do you have six silver denarii that you can pay me for this scroll?

"I'm sorry sir, but I'm only authorized to give you five silver denarii," Levi said as he held out his hand for the scroll.

Gabbai hesitated for a bit and then handed over the scroll. And then he takes a seat at Levi's table.

Levi took a scroll and broke the seal.

Gabbai complained, "You can't do that. Only the mediator Nicholaus can break that seal."

Levi assured Gabbai that he can open the seal and proceeded to examine the scroll. It was written in Greek. He asked as many questions as he thought he could get away with. After his close examination and copious note taking, he rolled up the scroll and placed it in his robe. He paid Gabbai his money, and Gabbai got up and departed, projecting an air of disgust, without saying another word.

Levi then goes to the Roman Room to find his master.

The Romans

There were people that could set at a table and carry on a conversation without the people at the next table hearing a word. And there were people whose whispers could be heard across the room. Marcus Gaius Manlius had a whisper that could be heard clear cross a mountain, and it was this booming voice that Nicholaus and everyone else hear shouting out, "Hail, Nicholaus, Awnee Ben-Adon, merchant of Tarsus and citizen of Rome."

In reply, Nicholaus raised his staff high over his head and then shouts as loud as he could, "Hail, Marcus Gaius Manlius, Roman centurion* of the Italian band, Tenth Fretensis Roman Legion, and citizen of Rome." Both men and all present then had a good hardy laugh.

Nicholaus mounted the platform where Marcus and his friends were seated. Greetings were continued, and wine was poured as the men made room for their visitor.

Nicholaus took his place among the Romans, and the small talk continued to the sound of the rattling of Tesserae* cups, the casting of lots*, and the shifting of coins a few tables over on the main floor. Lady curled up behind Nicholaus and laid her head upon her front paws. Marcus then directed a question to Nicholaus. "How do you sleep nights in this ungodly heat?"

"I am a full three score plus one years of age, and quite frankly, my friend, I sleep like a baby." After a pause, he continued, "I must have my afternoon nap, just like a baby, and I wake up in the middle of the night to tend to my physical needs."

The men all laughed.

"Yes, there are times when I wake up at night too," Marcus replied. "But my physical needs do not require the use of the chamber pot." Another round of laughter erupted in the room.

"Do you know Bar-Keziath*, the oil merchant? What can you tell me about him? I'm having a hard time trying to negotiate a deal with him for some olive oil."

Nicholaus smiled. "That, my dear Marcus, is because you don't know Bar-Keziath." Nicholaus leans forward. "Think of him with a bulla* around his neck. Bar-Keziath is from Galilee, the only son of his father. He has five older sisters. He and all his sisters look just like their mother, and you know how children look like the sexual aggressor at the time of their conception. Bar-Keziath's mother was a firstborn child and is the dominant member of her family. Bar-Keziath in turn married the firstborn of his mother's choosing. To successfully negotiate with Bar-Keziath, you must do so in the presence of his wife and then give them time to confer before you get an answer. Take a woman with you that speaks Aramaic. Give her all the information she will need as to quantity and quality delivery and the like, and then let her do all the negotiating. That way, you will make your deal and get your contract if you don't ask for more than they can produce and offer a fair price. Do as I say, my friend, and you will get your oil."

The small talk continued for a while, and then there was another question for Nicholaus. The centurion Cornelius, visiting down from Galilee, asked Nicholaus a question about the Hebrew law on divorce and remarriage. "It seems that King Herod Antipas the Tetrarch, has returned to Sepphoris* with a new wife. The religious leaders are privately having a fit over it."

"Who is this new wife? What can you tell me about her?"

"She is Herodias, divorced from King Philip and the granddaughter of Herod the Great. It seems that Antipas divorced his wife Phasaelis in order to marry her

"My dear friend Cornelius," Nicholaus smiled as he answered, "in Jewish Law, an unmarried man must marry his brother's widow as her kinsman redeemer*. But he cannot marry his brother's divorced wife. Under Hebrew law, the marriage you described is illegal. Such a marriage is adultery. By law, both the man and the woman must be tried under the testimony of two or more witnesses. If they are found to be guilty, they could be stoned to death. But I don't think it will come to that. Who in Sepphoris is going to bring a charge against the king and his wife?"

Another round of laughter ensued. The small talk continues to the amusement of all.

Cornelius then asked, "Tell me, my friend. As a citizen of Rome, what do you know of our Tenth Fretensis Legion?"

"Not much really. You were formed in about 712th or 713th year of Rome by Gaius Octavius. You fought in the war against Sextus Pompeius some six or so years later, and you put down the recent revolt in Galilee. Your toughness, endurance, and courage are known throughout the empire. Besides that, your wine is good, your conversation is stimulating, and it is always a joy to be in your company."

"Well said, my friend, well said."

The small talk continued, and in time Levi made his appearance. Lady got up to greet him. Nicholaus finished his drink and called out his apologies as he departed from the gathering of Roman officers, with Lady trailing behind.

Nicholaus and Levi walked back to their tables. Levi then gave Nicholaus the scroll and asked, "Why did you have me meet with this courier, Master?"

"You, my friend, were the price for his conceit and arrogance," Nicholaus said with a smile on his face. "I hope you made him earn his money. By the way, I am having something else to talk to you about. It concerns Eglah going to the market each morning without a male escort. I am concerned about her safety and about merchants taking advantage of her. Mistress Abishag discussed this with me, and I agree with her that Eglah needs an escort."

After some further discussion, Nicholaus asked Levi to escort Eglah every time she needed to go to the market. He could consider it as one of his regular duties.

Levi had a smile on his face when he said that he would be happy to.

My Wishes

In the year Marcus Vipsanius Agrippa first ruled in Syria, I, Awnee Ben-Adon, from Tarsus in Cilicia, was born a citizen of Rome. I am the son, both born and adopted, of Eubulus Cornelius Nicholaus, a merchant in Tarsus and citizen of Rome. My mother was Abigail Bat*-Leah, a Hebrew of the tribe of Dan, who was his indentured servant*.

Greetings to all who may have an interest in the dispensing of my positions and that which they may believe I possess at the time of my death.

Let it be known by all that in the fifteenth year of Tiberius Caesar, Pontius Pilatus governing in Judea, I have appointed Shimon Ben-Gamaliel to administer my wishes concerning all that some may feel it is mine at the time of my death. His decision in all related matters will be final. These are my wishes.*

I am a widower. I have no living offspring. My wife and my children all died of the fever many years ago. I never remarried or sired any more children.

My father is long deceased, and I have no brothers or sisters of record. I am the only child of my mother, who died giving birth to me. My father had no other children of record. There is no one related to me by blood that I would consider to be my family. Therefore there is no one to lay legal claim to any of my possessions by virtue of relationship. I have no living wife or living children, no indentured servants and no slaves. I only have my apprentice, Levi with a withered hand. I have no land or structures and no inheritance in Israel at the time of the Jubilee.

To my apprentice, Levi with a withered hand, I surrender the gifts I have laid aside for him. They are my table at Beth Eden, my library, my secure rooms, their scrolls, and all their other contents. All my pouches and their contents, all my writing materials, my working scrolls, and anything else that one might consider or contest as mine. All these are also his and his alone. They were my gifts to him held in trust until his time of need, or the time of my death, in recognition of his years of labor, love, and friendship, which he has bestowed upon me. I also charge him to use the secured pouches to settle all our accounts both his and mine under the direction of Shimon Ben-Gamaliel. It is to be understood that the decisions of Shimon Ben-Gamaliel are not to be questioned. They are final. These are my wishes.

It should be understood that all that is left over in the pouches or on the property or any place else, after the settling of our counts and filling all the rest of my bequeaths shall belong to Levi, with a withered hand, and him alone. These are my wishes.

To the sisters Mary Bat-Ruth, the wife of Sheva Ben-Benaiah of the tribe of Judah and Joann Bat-Ruth, the wife of Hantili the Hittite, and to their families, both of whom reside behind the shops in the north, across the street from Beth Eden, returned all their possessions that are in my rented rooms at their homes with the exception of the locked chest at the foot of my bed and its contents in my sleeping chamber, all my clothes, and any writing materials and scrolls that are there or in my study. The chest and all its contents, the writing materials, the scrolls, parchments, and such are the property of my apprentice, Levi with a withered hand, and are to be returned to him. The chest and the scrolls are not to be opened by anyone but him only. Each of the Bat-Ruth sisters is to receive 100 silver denarii from my pouches. These are my wishes.

To all who would wish to have retained my services, I leave my apprentice, Levi, with a withered hand. He is fluent in many languages, and I have trusted him with all that is mine for many years. He has learned well from me and has done much of my work for me in my latter years. He is worthy of your trust, and he will serve you well in the same spirit and with the same degree of honest and trustful service you have expected and received from me. These are my wishes.

To all the people I know, I leave my trust in the High Holy One of Israel as it is recorded in the writings, "Trust in Jehovah with all your heart, and lean not on your own understanding. In all your ways acknowledge him, and he shall direct your paths." [Prov. 3:5–6, from the Hebrew] I pray that you will place your trust in him and that he will guide you in all you say and do. Pray for peace in Jerusalem. These are my wishes.

I, Awnee Ben-Adon, from Tarsus of Cilicia, a Hebrew by birth and a citizen of Rome, attest to the contents of this scroll as being my final wishes in all the above by the affixing of my signet. This is a true expression of my final wishes concerning all that is mine at the time of my death.

Attested to as witness, by my signet, as a true expression of the wishes of Awnee Ben-Adon from Tarsus of Cilicia, a Hebrew and a citizen of Rome, in the above matter: Shimon-Ben Gamaliel, ruler of the Jews, member of the Sanhedrin* in Jerusalem.

He has a Greek copy of this, my last will and testament.

Attested to as witness by my signet as a true expression of the wishes of Awnee Ben-Adon from Tarsus of Cilicia, a Hebrew and a citizen of Rome, in the above matter: Marcus Gaius Manlius, Roman centurion of the Italian Band, Tenth Roman Legion, and Citizen of Rome.

He has a Greek copy of this, my Last Will and Testament.

5

The Offspring of Vipers

The route to Beth Eden, from the southwest section of the city, went north up past Herod's palace and the upper market. The route then continued east, to the west wall of the temple. Turning north and then west into the commercial area. Continue west to the three-storied building known as Beth Eden on the south side of the road.

Ben-Gorion followed the route in answer to his assignment. It is early in the morning, and he hoped no one would see him or hold his presence in Beth Eden against him. He was dressed as a common merchant with a pack on his back. As he traveled, he debated within himself if he should be purified after his encounter with *that Greek*.

Ben-Gorion entered Beth Eden and inquired for the mediator, Awnee Ben-Adon. Nicholaus rose from a nearby table and said, "I am Awnee Ben-Adon."

As Ben-Gorion approached the table, he found that Awnee Ben-Adon was a tall man of large stature with sloped shoulders. He was well kept and projecting an air of an upper-class Greek. Speaking in classic Hebrew, Ben-Gorion said, "I am Jonathan Ben-Gorion. I have been commissioned by the Council of the Ruling Elders of the Pharisees to be your contact with them."

Nicholaus pointed to the seat across from him and answered in classic Hebrew, "Good, I welcome you, Rabbi Jonathan Ben-

Gorion. I have been expecting you. Please help yourself to the food and wine."

Lady looked up at Ben-Gorion with a slight growl. Nicholaus patted her on the head and said, "It is all right, it is all right," and she lay back down.

Ben-Gorion was surprised at Ben-Adon's command of classic Hebrew. He was seated across from Nicholaus. He ignored the food and went right to business. "Tell me, Awnee Ben-Adon, do you have any scrolls for me?"

"Yes, we have one, which is all that has come up from the Jordan Valley." Turning to Levi, at the next table, he said to Ben-Gorion, "This is Levi, my apprentice." Then speaking to Levi in Greek, he said, "Levi, would you please retrieve the Baptist scroll that has been filed away? And go to the scroll room and bring me the Hebrew Isaiah scroll also."

Levi left their presence.

Nicholaus, now again speaking in perfect classic Hebrew, said to Ben-Gorion, "You must try the figs. They are exceptional and have freshly come from the market this morning. Or have an orange up from Jericho. They are as sweet as they can be. Have some bread and cheese. The bread is fresh baked this morning. Or try the wine, it is up from Byblus and mixed with honey. It takes a four-to-one cut very well."

Again Ben-Gorion turned down the offer as Nicholaus helped himself to a fig and a sip of wine.

Eglah came up to Levi's table and quietly sat herself. Lady came over, wagging all over, in her greetings. Eglah patted her head, scratched her ears, and gave her a good belly rub. Lady then got up and placed her paw on Nicholaus's lap. He pointed to the door and said, "Go." Lady trotted out the door on her twice-a-day mission to only she knew where to or what for.

There was awkward silence over the table as the men waited for Levi to return with the scrolls. Ben-Gorion got up from his chair, moved it over a bit, adjusted his cloak, and removed his backpack, which he placed on the floor. He then sat back down. Nicholaus on the other hand rearranged things on his table and then had another sip of wine. Eglah sensed the tension at the next table and was uncomfortable in the presence of Ben-Gorion.

Levi returned and handd the scrolls to Nicholaus. "Are these the scrolls you wanted, Master?"

Nicholaus looked the scrolls over and assured him that they were. Levi then took his seat with a big smile on his face for Eglah.

Nicholaus took the scrolls from Levi and thanked him for his services. He examined the scrolls again before handing one of them to Ben-Gorion. On the outside, it was labeled Baptist I.

Levi and Eglah excused themselves and left for the market. Ben-Gorion untied the scroll, opened it, and quickly read it.

Baptist I

Judas Ben Hakkatan, a Pharisee of Pharisees* of the tribe of Judah and servant of the High Holy one of Israel, blessed is he. To the Council of Ruling Elders in Jerusalem. Greetings and may the High Holy One of Israel, blessed is he, bless and keep you. Amen.

In obedience to your wish for us to observe and report on activities of the Baptist, the following observations are hereby submitted for your approval.

When I found the Baptist, he was standing knee deep in the water of a cove of the Jordan River. He looked like a wild man and was dressed in camel's hair with a leather girdle about his waist. He looked unkempt and had an offensive odor about him.

He was preaching, "Repent for the kingdom of the heavens has drawn near." He was also preaching a need to be baptized for the remission of sins.

Many people are going out to hear him, and some are confessing their sins and being baptized. Some of these people being baptized are Pharisees* while others are Levites Minor Scribes* and minor priests.

When some of the minor priests came to see what was happening, he called them the offspring of vipers. Then he said, "Who has warned you to flee from the coming wrath? Produce fruits worthy of repentance. Do not think to say within yourselves that we have a father Abraham. For I say to you, the High Holy One of Israel is able to rise up children to Abraham from these stones. Already the ax is even laid to the root of the trees; therefore, any tree not producing good fruit is cut down and thrown into the fire. If you have two tunics, give one to the one that has none, and if you have food share it with them." [Matt. 3:5–10 and Luke 3:7–9 from the Greek]

A publican* asked what he should do. The Baptist's answered that he was not to collect more than was required. [Luke 3:10–12 from the Greek]

I saw Zacchaeus, the chief of publicans in Jericho, and I asked him what he thought about the Baptist's advice. He said that the quality of the advice depended on who was determining "what was required."

Some soldiers asked him what they should do. He said to not exhort money, don't accuse people falsely, and be content with their pay. [Luke 3:14 from the Greek]

I have nothing more to report at this time.

Be it known to all that I have entrusted this scroll to my slave Gabbai of the tribe of Benjamin for transport to the Council of Ruling Elders in Jerusalem and to act in my name.

The Lord bless you and keep you. The Lord make His face to shine upon you and be gracious to you. The Lord lift up his countenance upon you and give you peace. [Num. 6:24–26 from the Hebrew]

Ben-Gorion places the scroll in his robe and pays Nicholaus for it. He then says, "Tell me, Awnee Ben-Adon, what do you think about this Baptist?"

"There's too little information here about the Baptist to make a judgment," Nicholaus replied. "But I did find it interesting that he came to a land of country peasants, wandering sheep, and wild beast to proclaim his message instead of coming to the temple here in Jerusalem. His speech is fearless and filled with a sense of reproof for sin and demanding acts of repentance.

Ben-Gorion paused for a few seconds. "What about the contents of the scrolls?"

"The reference to the kingdom of heavens is interesting and may be a reference to the renewed kingdom of David. I'm going to have to study it before I can give a more detailed reply to that question. His reference to offspring of vipers may be a reference to the serpent in the garden of Eden or a serpentine-like motive behind their coming to see him. The 'stones' may be the twelve stones Joshua took out of the midst of the Jordan or the stony hearts of the repentant as recorded in Ezekiel. 'The ax laid to the root of the trees' is most likely a reference to some coming judgment of the individuals present or of the movements they are representing as is the reference to fire—again more study is needed. The instruction to share food and tunics reflects the wishes of the High Holy One of Israel, blessed is his name, for us to do good deeds for the poor. The writer does not indicate if the soldiers are Jewish or Roman. But if they are Roman, the indications are that repentance, baptism, and the remission of sins are available to the Gentiles. As I read the scrolls, I was reminded of a passage in the Isaiah Scroll." He takes up the Isaiah scroll and opens it. He reads aloud, "Comfort, oh comfort my people says the Holy One of Israel, blessed is he. Speak you priests to the heart of Jerusalem, comfort her for her humiliation is accomplished that her sin is put away, for she has received of the Lord's hand double the amount of her sins. 'The voice of one crying in the wilderness, 'Prepare you the way of the Lord make straight paths for the holy one of Israel, blessed is he. Every valley shall be filled and every mountain and hill shall be brought low, and all the crooked ways shall become straight and the rough places plain and the glory of the Lord shall appear and all flesh shall see the salvation of the Holy One of Israel, Blessed is He. For the Lord has spoken it.'" [Isaiah 40:1b–5 from the Hebrew]

Nicholaus then rolls up the Isaiah scroll and places it on the table. "There are two other things. This Baptism is not a repeated act, but a one-time-only act to repentance. He is leveling class distinction. He has reduced everyone to one common ground. I have nothing else to report. I have written all this down in another commentary scroll for you."

Ben-Gorion studies Nicholaus for a long moment, and then he pays him his dues. "I will be back this time next week." With this, he stands up and leaves.

The Mikveh

Ben-Gorion departed from Beth Eden in a hurry. He turned right onto the road that was leading east, to the Antonia Fortress, then south to a long narrow building on the east side of the road, between the road and the west wall of the temple. This was the headquarters of the Council of the Ruling Elders of the Pharisees.

Ben-Gorion entered by the north entrance and headed for the Mikveh*, just inside the door. The attendant took his backpack and helped him disrobe and entered the bath as they recited a prayer for purification. After completion of the ritual, Ben-Gordon made a second pass through the bath. The attendant helped him put on his Pharisee's robe, his Tallit Gadol*, and Tefillins*. Then Ben-Gorion, with backpack in hand, headed for the office of the Council Secretary.

Ben-Gorion arrived at the office of the council secretary to find the secretary and Ben-Gamaliel waiting for him. Abner Ben-Hilkiah, the council secretary, got up from his chair to greet Ben-Gorion, as did Ben-Gamaliel. Then Ben-Gorion returned greetings to both of the men.

The three men ritually washed their hands and then helped themselves to the food and wine laid out for them on a separate table. Ben-Gamaliel, being senior, prays over the food and the gathering for himself and the other two men.

Ben-Gorion then produced the scroll, and all three men went over it in detail as they enjoyed their meal together.

Ben-Gamaliel was the first to react to the reading. "Did you note the boldness with which the Baptist addresses the minor priests? He speaks to them as 'a generation of vipers.' He doesn't care who was offended by his words."

"Yes, and how plain and to the point his words were. There is no question about his feelings about them," noted the secretary.

"He also exposes the uselessness of repentance, which is not accompanied by a change in lifestyle. 'Bring forth fruit worthy of repentance.' Being baptized just to please is not going to make it," Ben-Gorion added.

"Tell me, Jonathan, what did Nicholaus have to say about the Baptist?" Ben-Gamaliel asked.

"Nothing really. He said he did not have enough information yet to make a judgment."

Abner Ben-Hilkiah then asked, "What about the symbolism?"

"Just the pat answers that you would expect anyone to give. With the exception of the soldiers. He said the soldiers were not identified as to being Jewish or Roman, and then he suggested that if they are Roman, the Baptist thinks that the forgiveness of sins is available to the Gentile for the price of repentance and baptism. He said that he thinks the teachings of the Baptist are doing away with class distinction. He has reduced everyone to one common ground. He doesn't have any respect for office or position. He will not be making many friends among the Sadducees."

The men think about this for a moment, and then Abner Ben-Hilkiah suggests that he would send a message to Ben-Zadok, who is in Jordan, to ask him about the soldiers and the way he was received by the population in general. "We should pass everything else on to the Council for their evaluation."

The men then agreed that this was a good plan.

Ben-Gamaliel then asked, "Did you have any other impressions you would like to share with us?'

Ben-Gorion replied, "Only that I thought it was inappropriate for Judas to approach Zaccheus as he did. But the council can deal with that."

Abner Ben-Hilkiah then paid Ben-Gorion his due, and they finished their meal together. After the meal, Abner went about his duties as the other two men left together.

Home

Across the street and directly north of Beth Eden were two buildings that were connected to each other and featuring three front doors. The building served as a dividing line between the pottery district to the west and the clothing district to the east. The west door led to a potter's shop with living quarters in the back. This was the home of Sheva Ben-Benaiah of the tribe of Judah, his wife, Mary, and their son Chilion, who was born blind. The east door led to the garment, leather, and carpenter's shop. It also had living quarters in the back. This was the home of Hantili the Hittite and his wife, Joann. On the ground floor, the buildings were divided by a narrow alley closed in the front, with a door to the outside. Inside was a narrow stairs on the left side leading to the second floor and a passageway leading to a courtyard in back, shared by the two buildings. From the front it looks like one building with three doors. There was a sign over the east and west outside doors indicating the wares within.

In the late afternoon, Nicholaus and Levi closed up shop, moved everything to the secure areas west of the public area, and then went their separate ways. Lady ran on ahead and waited at the door for Nicholaus. Nicholaus then took up his staff and worked his way across the road to the home of the sisters Mary and Joann. Entering the center door, he was greeted with the aroma of lentil stew and of fresh baked bread for the evening sup. One of the servant girls rushed up to him with a basin and a towel to wash his feet. Lady ran to the kitchen, where Mary ha a dish prepared for her. A table had been set in the adjoining courtyard, and all was ready for the extended family's evening meal. Nicholaus found the food to be excellent and the idle conversation of the evening meal to be soothing after a long day's work.

After the evening meal, Nicholaus and the two other men retired to the roof for their nightly men's time together, with Lady tailing behind.

A table had been prepared in the center of the roof courtyard with oranges, dried fruit, goblets, and a wineskin of five-to-one cut wine mixed with honey. Each of the men had a chair that Hantili built just for them. Small talk about the events of the day was the normal conversation.

Nicholaus started the conversation by recounting their encounter with Gabbai. This started a general conversation about the Baptist. Sheva said that he thought the Baptist was just another Zealot,* and Hantili said that he couldn't keep up with the complexities of all of these Jewish prophets.

Sheva then asked Nicholaus if he knew anything about a Levite named Bar-Shual.

"Yes," said Nicholaus. "One of the foxes of Galilee. He reminds me of the chicken who thought the sun has risen in the morning just to hear him crow. Think of the ridicule and knavery of a Syrian robber and the savageness of an Egyptian mercenary, a despot* in the making, and you will have some idea of what you are dealing with. Bar-Shual is a chore boy for the temple priests, and I wouldn't trust him for anything but trouble."

"Well, he came into the shop today to price some pots. He didn't place an order or buy anything, but he said he might be back."

Nicholaus considered the situation for a short while and then said, "Let me work up some blank contracts for you to have him sign if he comes back to place an order. I will make two copies. Have someone witness both of you signing both copies. Be sure to list each item he wants in detail. Quote him a price that is half again higher than you would normally charge. This will either scare him off or make his aggravation worth your while."

"Thank you, friend Nicholaus, that should help the situation, but all in all, I'd be happy if he just never came back again."

Sheva then remarked that Chilion had a birthday coming up in a week. "Now we will have another man in the house."

Hantili said that Joann had been reminding him of it every day and that he had already started a new chair for him.

Then Sheva reflected that if he knew Mary, there would be a big birthday celebration that was in the planning stages already. "Family and friends will be coming from all over, and our nightly wine will be cut six to one, with an extra measure of honey."

Evening shadows rose up from the depths of the city, and night was upon the gathering. Nicholaus said, "The time has come for me to allow my body to lie down and rest, to allow my mind to go out and play and let my soul commune with God." With that he excuses himself. He and Lady go to his rooms to go to bed. She curls up behind his knees.

The Sandal Man

Ben-Gorion arrived at Beth Eden much later than his usual time.

Levi and Eglah entered right behind him. Eglah ran upstairs with her packages as Levi went to his table.

Ben-Gorion went to the table of Nicholaus. Lady looked up and then lay back down. Nicholaus stood to give him the proper Jewish greeting, offering him some morning bread and fruit. Ben-Gorion turned down the favor and, as usual, went right to business: "Do you have any scrolls for me this week?"

"Yes, just one." Turning to Levi, he asked him to hand him the Baptist scroll they just finished and to retrieve the Hebrew Deuteronomy scroll and the Isaiah scroll also.

Nicholaus took the Baptist scroll and handed it to Ben-Gorion. Levi then hurried off to get the other two. On the outside it was labeled Baptist II. Ben-Gorion untied the scroll, opened, and quickly read it.

Baptist II

I, Abiathar Ben-Zadok of Jericho, born a Pharisee, send you greetings in the name of my father who is a member of your council.

My father instructed me to find the Baptist and to report to you what I saw him do and heard him say.

I found the Baptist along the Jordan. These are the things I heard him say when a delegation of minor priests and Levites from the temple came to question him.

He told them that he is not the Christ.

They question him further. They asked him if he was Elijah, and he said that he was not.

"Are you the prophet?"

And he answered, "No."

Then they said, "Who are you then, that we may give an answer to those who sent us?"

He said, "I am a voice crying in the wilderness, make the way of the Lord straight." [John 1:19–23 from the Greek]

Afterward, I asked him, "Why do you baptize if you are not the Christ or Elijah or the Prophet?"

He said that he baptized with water, but one who stands in your midst whom you do not know, he it is who comes after me, who has been before me, of whom I am not worthy that I should untie the latchet of his sandal. [John 1:24–27 from the Greek]

Ben-Gorion looked up from the scroll at Nicholaus and then found his place and went back to reading.

I sent my servants Abihail and Rizpah, who were with me attending to my needs, down to be baptized. I told them to ask if he was the anointed one of Israel. The following is their testimony.

"We asked the Baptist if he was the anointed one of Israel. He said he was not. Then he said that he baptized with water to repentance, but there was one to follow that is more powerful, whose sandals he was not fit to carry. He will baptize you in the Holy Spirit and fire. His fan is in his hand, and he cleanses his floor and will gather his wheat into the barn. But he will burn up the chaff with fire that cannot be put out. He then said we should find this man and do whatever he tells us to do." [Luke 3:16–17 from the Greek]

.Ben-Gorion looked up again and then continued reading.

The next day, I saw the Baptist pointing into the crowd and exclaim, "Behold, the Lamb of God, who takes away the sin of the world!" I looked to see who he was talking about, but I could not pick him out of the crowd. [John 1:29 from the Greek]

I have nothing more to report, and I trust this will satisfy my father's request.

The Lord bless you and keep you. The Lord make His face to shine upon you and be gracious to you. The Lord lift up his countenance upon you and give you peace. [Num. 6:24–26 from the Hebrew]

Ben-Gorion laid the scroll down and looked across the table at Nicholaus. With a tremor in his voice, he asked, bewildered, "There is another one to follow that is more powerful?" He asked with a bewildering look on his face. "Who is this sandal man? Who is this Lamb of God?"

Nicholaus smiled at Ben-Gordon and replied that he did not know. He went on to say, "I am now satisfied the Baptist does not believe himself to be the Messiah nor the prophet foretold by Moses. His answer to the various questions leads me to believe that he is an Essene* or at least has been influenced by their teachings. As to the sandal man, there is a passage in Deuteronomy that may be of value to you."

Levi handed the Deuteronomy scroll to Nicholaus as Ben-Lahad, the jeweler, joined them at Levi's table.

Nicholaus opened the scroll to the place he had marked and began reading aloud. "I will raise up to them a prophet of their brethren like you (Moses), and I will put my words in his mouth and he shall speak to them as I shall command him. Whatever man shall not hearken to whatsoever words the Prophet shall speak, in my name, I will take vengeance on him. But the prophet whosoever shall impiously speak in my name a word which I have not commanded him to speak and whosoever shall speak in the name of other gods, that prophet shall die. But if you shall say in your heart, 'How shall we know the word which the Lord has not spoken?' Whatsoever words that prophet shall speak in the name of the Lord and they shall not come true and not come to pass, this is the thing which the Lord has not spoken and the prophet has spoken wickedly. You shall not spare him." (Deut. 18:18–22 from the Hebrew)

Nicholaus then handed the scroll back to Levi, and Levi handed him the Isaiah scroll.

"As to the 'Lamb of God', I found this passage in Isaiah." Unrolling the scroll, he begins to read. "Oh Lord, who has believed our report? And to whom has the arm of the Lord been revealed? We brought a report as of a child before him; he is a root in a thirsty land: he has no form nor comeliness; and we saw him, but he had no form nor beauty. But his form was ignoble and inferior to that of the children of men; he was a man in suffering, an acquainted with the bearing of sickness, for his face is turned from us; he was dishonored, and not esteemed. He bears our sins and pained for us: yet we accounted him to be in trouble, and in suffering, and in affliction. But he was wounded on account of our sins, and was bruised because of our iniquities: the chastisement of our peace was upon him; and by his bruises we were healed. All we as sheep have gone astray; everyone has gone astray in his way; and the Lord gave him up for our sins". (Isaiah 53:1-6 from the Hebrew)

"I was also reminded of Abraham, when he told his son Isaac that the High Holy One would provide Himself a lamb for a burnt offering" (Gen. 22:7 from the Hebrew).

"As to the rest of the scroll, I think that Abiathar Ben-Zadok is a poor example of a Pharisee, and his father has a large problem on his hands." Nicholaus then handed him his commentary scroll.

Ben-Gorion had a troubled and bewildered look on his face as he paid for the scroll and quickly got up to leave.

Nicholaus, Levi, and Ben-Lahad continued discussing the situation, and Ben Lahad gave Levi his request for contracts.

*****

Ben-Gorion hurried to the council chambers. He bypassed the ritual bath and the donning of his Pharisees robe. There he was met by Abner Ben-Hilkiah and Ben-Gamaliel. He eagerly shared the second scroll with them. Ben-Gamaliel read the scroll quickly and handed it to Abner. Then he asked Jonathan what Nicholaus thought about the Baptist.

Jonathan said that Nicholaus thought the Baptist was not the Messiah but that he might be an Essene.

"What about the sandal man?" Abner asked.

Jonathan replied, "Nicholaus had no opinion as to the sandal man, but he quoted a passage from Isaiah to explain the Lamb of God. The passage that he quoted was the 'All we like sheep have gone astray' passage. Maybe we should have Ben-Zadok follow up on the sandal man and see what he can find out."

Abner and Ben-Gamaliel looked at each other and nodded in agreement. Abner said he would report the scroll and his findings to the council. After that, he paid Jonathan his due, and both Jonathan and Gamaliel left the building.

I Saw Him

The following week, Ben-Gorion again found his way to Ben-Adon's table. Lady looked up, sniffed the air, and then laid back down.

Nicholaus greeted Ben-Gorion and made his usual offer of food and drink. He then assured him that there were no new scrolls.

Ben-Gorion sat down and said, "I would just as soon set here for a while if you don't mind. The priests have run all of the teachers out of the Court of the Gentiles for Passover. They say there are two to three hundred thousand or more worshipers expected in the city for Passover. That means they're going to have to sacrifice up to thirty thousand lambs and kids this week. They have brought all twenty-four courses of the priests into the temple to handle the sacrifices, plus all the herds, flocks, and all the moneychangers. There's just no place to put them all, so they have taken over the court of the Gentiles for the overflow. I had to cancel my class because I don't have any place left to gather them together and to teach them."

Nicholaus replied, "I understand the situation. That's why the priest needed so many money pots to sell to the moneychangers. The centurion Manlius told me that the Romans are going to clean out the prison of all the malcontents and crucify them along the road outside the Damascus gate. This is supposed to show the travelers that Rome is still in charge. According to Manlius, 'Even Roman law will not secure the happiness of a people whose manners are universally corrupt, but Roman crucifixion will protect the Just.' Quite frankly, I'll be glad when it's all over. I appreciate the remembrance of Passover, but the atmosphere created by the priest and the Romans is not very conducive to worship."

"Fire, water, and governments know nothing of mercy," Ben-Gorion observed.

As the men were talking, two more men approach the table. Nicholaus recognized one of them as the Pharisee Baruch Bar-Azariah from Galilee. Nicholaus and Ben-Gorion stood up to give greetings to the newcomers. Levi surrendered his two chairs and slid his table over to that of Nicholaus so everyone could be seated comfortably.

Bar-Azariah then introduced his eldest son, Dodai, and explained that this was his first trip to Jerusalem as a salesman. He then requested that Nicholaus explained to him the procedures for contracts and mediation.

Nicholaus explained that contracts were drawn up between buyers and sellers, detailing all the items agreed to. Each buyer and each seller would have a copy of the contract in his own language. A third copy in Greek was retained by the mediator. Contracts detailed all the conditions of the agreement. If there was a dispute, in the execution of the contract, the mediator and the Greek scroll were the final judges as to who would do what according to the contracts.

The men then had a short time of small talk, and then Bar-Azariah gave Nicholaus his list of contracts. Then he and his son excused themselves.

*****

A little later, Jada Ben-Lahad, the jeweler, came rushing up to the table. "I saw him!" he shouted. Lady jumps up in fright and then cowers behind Nicholaus. "I think I saw your sandal man."

Ben-Lahad then settled down and explained, "I was in the temple, in the Court of Israel, and there was a commotion in the Court of the Gentiles. I went out to see what was happening, and I saw a man driving the sheep and oxen out of the temple. He was being cheered on by some of the people as he was tipping over the money pots and overturning the tables of the moneychangers. He released the sacrificial doves and shouted something about a house of merchandise. It was quite a sight to see" [John 2:14–16 from the Greek].

Nicholaus and Ben-Gorion are both surprised at Ben-Lahad's declaration.

Ben-Gorion got up and said that he must go to the council chambers to see what their reaction was going to be. And he hurriedly departed.

Nicholaus asked Levi to interview Ben-Lahad and to write up what he saw and heard and add it to their collection of council scrolls.

For the rest of the day, all of Beth Eden was abuzz with tales of the events in the temple. There were all kinds of rumors and speculations as to just who the man was and what it was all about. Nicholaus could not help but think about a passage in Malachi: "Behold, I am sending my messenger, and he will clear the way before me. And the Lord whom you are seeking shall suddenly come to his Temple, even the Angel of the covenant, in whom you delight. Behold, he comes, says Jehovah of hosts. But who can endure the day of his coming? And who will stand when he appears? For he is like a refiners fire, and a fuller's, soap. And he shall sit as a refiner and purifier of silver; and he shall purify the sons of Levi, and purge them like gold and like silver, that they may be offered as a food offering in righteousness to Jehovah" (Malachi 3:1–3 from the Hebrew).

*****

Late the next day, Nicholaus and Levi were still at their tables when Ben-Gorion returned.

Coming up to the table, Ben-Gorion said, "I have news. The man in the temple was Jesus of Nazareth. The council has convened to discuss the situation. It seems that this Jesus charged the priest with making his father's house a house of merchandise. He was then challenged as to what he was doing. They said to him, 'What sign do you show to us since you do these things?' Jesus said to them, 'Destroy this temple, and in three days I will raise it up.' Then the

Jews said, 'This temple took forty-six years to build, and you would raise it up in three days?'" (John 2:16–20 from the Greek).

"The question went unanswered and the council has prevailed on me to seek out the Nazarene and interview him. They think that anyone who can defy the priest like that is interesting enough to be interviewed and asked to join us. It is believed that he can be found in the garden of Gethsemane, on Mount of Olives. I am to go there to seek him out and interview him. I would like both of you to come with me as my witnesses and record all you see and hear. Oh, there is one other thing, when you write this up, use my Greek name."

Levi then said, "But, Master, what is your Greek name?"

Ben-Gorion replied, "My Greek name is Nicodemus."

Recap

L evi had told Eglah that he could not go to the market because of the scrolls he had to work on. He had gone directly to the security rooms to receive his scrolls.

Eglah decided to go alone. She had a whole list of things to get that just could not wait.

Ben-Gorion had a quick pace as he headed for Beth Eden. He was about to receive the report of his interview with the Nazarene. He was anxious and concerned about its content and accuracy and how it was going to be received by the Council of Elders.

Ben-Gorion went directly to the table of Nicholaus and was thankful there was no one there ahead of him. The usual greetings were exchanged, along with an offer of food and drink. Then Ben-Gorion seated himself and asked about Levi, who was conspicuously absent.

Nicholaus said that Levi was gathering up scrolls, and he would be with them momentarily.

Ben-Gorion then asked Nicholaus, "What did you think about your encounter with the Nazarene?"

Nicholaus thought for a moment and said that the Nazarene was either the most articulate charlatan he has ever seen or a prophet of God.

Ben Gorion then asked, "Do you think he is the Messiah?"

"I don't know, but he teaches with a degree of authority that I have never witnessed before."

Levi approached the table with an arm full of scrolls. He laid the scrolls out on his table and then selected four of them to give to Nicholaus. "I have produced four copies of my report, one for each one of us and one for the council."

Nicholaus gave two of the scrolls to Ben-Gorion and one of them back to Levi. The men unrolled their scrolls and began to read as Levi moves his chair over to Nicholaus' table.

"I hope I covered everything, but I think we ought to review the whole report, in case I missed something."

Levi I

There was a man of the Pharisees, Nicodemus is his name, a ruler of the Jews. This one came to Jesus by night and said to him, "Rabbi, we know that you have come as a teacher from God. For no one is able to do those miracles which you do, except God be with him."

Jesus answered and said to him, "Truly, truly I say to you, if one does not receive birth from above, he is not able to see the Kingdom of God."

Nicodemus said to him, "How is a man able to be born, being old? He is not able to enter into his mother's womb a second time and be born?"

Jesus answered, "Truly, truly I say to you, if one does not receive birth out of water and the spirit, he is not able to enter into the Kingdom of God. That receiving birth from the flesh is flesh, and that receiving birth from the spirit is spirit. Do not wonder because I told you 'You must receive birth from above.' The spirit breezes where he desires, and you hear his voice, but you do not know from where he comes and where he goes. So is everyone having received birth from the spirit."

Nicodemus answered and said to him, "How can these things come about?"

> Jesus answered and said to him, "You are the teacher of Israel, and you do not know these things? Truly, truly I say to you. That which we know, we speak; and that which we have seen, we testify. And you do not receive our testimony. If I tell you earthly things and you do not believe, how will you believe if I tell you heavenly things? And no one has gone up into heaven except he having come down out of heaven, the Son of Man who is in heaven.
>
> "And even as Moses lifted up the serpent in the wilderness, so must the Son of Man be lifted up that everyone believing in him should not perish but have everlasting life. For God so loved the world that he gave his only begotten son that everyone believing into him should not perish, but have everlasting life. For God did not send his son into the world that he might judge the world but that the world might be saved through him. The one believing into him is not judged, but the one not believing has already been judged; for he has not believed into the name of the only begotten Son of God.
>
> "And this is the judgment, that the light has come into the world, and man loved the darkness more than the light, for their works are evil. For everyone practicing wickedness hates the light and does not come to the light that his works may not be exposed. But the one doing the truth comes to the light, that his works may be revealed, that they have been worked in God (John 3:1–21 from the Greek).

Ben-Gorion spoke up first. "At first reading, I think you covered everything. You are to be congratulated for a job well done."

"Thank you, Master. I appreciate your complement."

Ben-Gorion said, "You are welcome, Levi, and it's just the three of us here, so call me Nicodemus. Tell me, Levi: What did you think of the prophet?"

Levi thought for a moment and said, "My first impression was on how he looked. I could not have picked him out from amongst his followers. If he had not come out to us, I would have never been able to identify him. I was also impressed with his articulation of the Hebrew language. If I had closed my eyes, I would have never guessed he was a Galilean."

Nicodemus then added, "I was surprised about the way he dodged the implied question in my opening greeting to him. It was as if he knew I was coming and went directly to what he wanted to say to me." He then reached over and helped himself to a fig.

Nicholaus then said, "I was interested in the different ways he referred to himself: the Son of Man and the Light. And was his reference to 'the only begotten Son of God' about himself or someone else? And what about that going up into and coming down from heaven? As I read that, I was reminded of a passage in Proverbs. I think I can remember it. 'Who has gone up to heaven or come down? Who has gathered the wind to his fist? Who has bound the waters in a garment? Who has made all the ends of the earth to rise? What is his name, and what is his son's name? Surely you know'" (Prov. 30:4 from the Hebrew).

Levi then said that he did not understand the illustration about Moses lifting up the serpent.

Nicholaus rolled up his scroll and excused himself, saying, "I don't know the answers to your questions, but I'm going to take them all to the council." With that, he left Beth Eden and headed for the council chambers.

Gods, Gods, and More Gods

The week passed quickly. Everyone was resting up after Passover. At the urging of Nicholaus, the sisters Mary and Joann had invited Levi and Eglah to celebrate the Passover with their families. This seemed most appropriate sense as they were so close to Nicholaus and had no families of their own.

The sisters could not help but notice the extra attention Eglah and Levi were paying to each other.

*****

The festivities were over. Twenty-three of the courses of priests and what was left of the extra flocks and the herds along with the moneychangers had been dismissed and sent back home, and things were getting back to normal.

Levi came in with Eglah and helped her up the stairs with her packages. He then came down and hurried back to the security rooms where he gathered up the materials he needed for the day's project.

Levi returned from his trip to the security room. He had a young lad with him. Levi introduced him as Daniel Bar-Ananiel of the tribe of Naphtali. He is a new mediator, who has a table along the back wall.

Nicholaus got up from his chair and welcomed the new mediator. The three men sat down and had a leisure time of refreshment and getting acquainted with each other. Levi then went back to Daniel's table with him for more conversation.

When he returned, he saw the centurions Manlius and Cornelius. The centurions were in native dress, as was their habit when they wished to circulate in public without arousing attention. But he could not help but notice the outline of the short swords at their hips.

Levi set about doing his chores for the day, but he overheard the conversation Nicholaus was having with the centurions.

Manlius was saying, "Our engineers can do the impossible. Trust me, if we can cross any sea or any terrain, we can take any fortification. Jerusalem and even Masada can be taken if the need ever arises."

"I would like to meet one of your engineers," Nicholaus replied. "I would like him to teach me how to break bread without making any crumbs."

All three had a good laugh.

Then Cornelius changed subjects by saying, "The weather people are telling us that this was going to be an unusually warm winter."

Nicholaus replied, "I hope not. The last time we had an unusually warm winter, I was so sick I thought I was going to die. I was in bed for about two weeks, and the sisters had to take care of me. My chest was so heavy I thought a beast of some kind the setting on it. The pressure in my head was almost unbearable. I was coughing up oysters. The sisters would beat on my back to help me loosen up the congestion. First, I would shiver, and then I would sweat. I got very little sleep, and I couldn't eat a thing. It hurt to swallow, and it even hurt to breathe. I could hardly move. I was the most miserable I have ever been in my entire life."

Manlius then asked, "Why didn't you pray to the gods? Maybe your sickness would not have lasted so long."

Nicholaus sat back in his chair and thought for a second, and then he said, "You and the Greeks have gods, gods, and more gods.

I don't know how you keep up with them all. Tell me, just which of the gods do you suggest that I should have prayed to?"

Cornelius was the first to answer, "My choice would be Vejovis, the god of healing, or Febris, the goddess who embodies and protects people from the fever."

"Don't forget Carna, the goddess who is presiding over the heart and other organs," Manlius added.

"Tell me, of all the gods, which ones do you worship?"

Manlius thought for a moment and then answered, "For me, there are three basic groups that I consider. First and foremost are the politically expedient, second the ones that are most popular, and last but not least, the ones that bring me joy, comfort, and pleasure. Now tell me about your god or gods."

At this point, Levi set aside his project and opened a clean parchment thinking this may be worth recording.

Nicholaus thought for a moment and then replied, "I only have one God that has three personalities, but really four. Before the beginning of time and the creation as we know them, there was an Extreme Being, the first personality. This being lives in spheres of existence, which are beyond our comprehension. These spheres are as foreign and expansive as an elephant is to an ant. This Extreme Being conceived of two new parallel spheres of existence, one spiritual, as we understand spiritual, and the other physical, as we understand physical.

He separated aside a part of himself, the first separated per-sonality, to be his spiritual self in the spiritual existence as Extreme Ruler over both the physical and spiritual. He separated out a second portion of himself to be the second separated personality, to be his physical self in both the spiritual and physical existence, and to rule over the physical. He then separated out a third portion of himself to be the third separated personality, to be his spiritual presence in both the spirit and physical existence and to hold the office of the active agent, in the physical, for the other two. The first of these new personalities I understand to be God the Father. The second is God the King of kings and Lord of lords, and the third is God the Spirit. God the Father is outside of time as we understand time. For him, everything is right now past, present, and future. He is the all-knowing God."

Waving his arms over his head, Cornelius then asked, "Then how did all of this come about?"

Nicholaus again thought for a moment and replied, "The three new personalities are not only in continuous communications with each other but also in a state of complete togetherness. Before the beginning, the God the Spirit was hovering over the totally dark chaos of complete nothingness. God the King of kings said to God the Spirit, 'Let there be light.' God the Spirit then took the spoken word of God the King of kings and, out of the power of that spoken word, created light. This light is not light as we understand it. It is the complete opposite of the totally dark chaos of nothingness the Holy Spirit had been hovering over. This light would be the spirit world as we understand it. God the Father then saw the light and saw that it was good, and God the King of kings then caused the God the Spirit to divide the light from the darkness. He then called the light Day and the darkness Night, so this became the evening and the morning of the first day of creation.

"On the second day, they created the heavens overhead. On the third day, they caused dry land to appear and they called it Earth. Then they caused the Earth to be filled with all of the seed bearing plants and trees according to its kind. On the fourth day, they created the Stars, and The Sun and the Moon to mark the seasons and to rule over the day and the night. On the fifth day they created all the sea creatures and the birds that fly above the earth. On the sixth day they created all of the animals and man, both male and female, and charged them to be fruitful and multiply and fill the earth and subdue it and to have dominion over all. On the seventh day God rested."

Cornelius said, "Okay, but then where did all your laws come from?"

Levi smiled and thought to himself, "This ought to be interesting."

Nicholaus then explained, "Israeli law has three primary sources. The first is the Torah*, the writings of Moses, known as the Law of

49

Moses. The sacrifices required by the Law of Moses were fulfilled when Solomon's Temple was completed, and temple worship was established."

"The Written Law came about during the Babylonian captivity. The temple was gone, as was the priesthood. The Rabbis in Babylon established written laws for the people so that they may continue worshiping God. This is known as the Babylonian Talmud* or the Written Law."

"The verbal refinement of the Written Law, or the Mishnah*, has its beginning shortly after the death of Moses, and has been an ongoing conversation ever since. The Oral Law is a refining conversation amongst Rabbis that has no end in sight."

"I am satisfied that it was the intent of God the Father to give man his laws so that man might have a fuller, happier, more complete, and productive life. I am also satisfied that the Commandments and the law of Moses are sufficient to that end and that the Babylonian Talmud and the Mishnah and all the other ones about the law are nothing more than man's interfering with the Law of Moses and the will of God the Father."

The line of people waiting to see Nicholaus came to the attention of the centurions. With this, they excused themselves and walked away, talking to each other in the language neither Nicholaus nor Levi recognized.

12

I Am Not the Christ

The market was abuzz with merchants setting up their tables with the new merchandise that had just arrived by caravan from the east. Adding to the turmoil, Ben-Merari and his entourage were oppressing and persecuting the merchants for dealing with sinners. It was their lot in life to enforce all the laws of Israel and to make life as miserable as possible for everyone who wasn't a Pharisee. Merchants were a low-life captive audience that was ripe for the picking. The merchants could not avoid them, and neither could the beggars or other assorted apparent servants and assumed lower-class shoppers.

Levi was enjoying the stewpot-like assortment of aromas he smelled coming from the food vendors as he searched for Eglah. He found her looking at fabrics that had just arrived by caravan. The ladies were always interested in new fabrics that can be made into items to allure their patrons. They also liked trinkets and inexpensive jewelry that were always of interest, along with the latest news and gossip that circulated freely throughout the market.

Eglah was eager to see Levi and took his arm as they meandered on through the market. She had to stop at nearly every display and look for hidden treasures. Levi stopped at a food vendor and purchased two warm pita breads filled with leaks, goat cheese, and chopped olives. He gave one to Eglah and kept the other for himself. He then stopped a wandering wine dispenser for two cups of wine that had been cut five to one but with no added honey. They enjoyed their food, wine, and each other's company as they continued with Eglah's shopping.

*****

Nicodemus was getting discouraged as he made his weekly track to Beth Eden. He wondered if maybe the Pharisees down in the valley did not understand the urgency of the council's request for information. Or maybe they lacked enough motivation and incentive to get out and retrieve it and then send it up to them. Upon entering Beth Eden, he went directly to Ben-Adon's table.

Lady looked up and then lay back down.

Nicholaus rose to greet his guest. "Welcome, my friend. Settle down. Help yourself to the food and drink. Levi and Eglah are not back from the market yet, but I have good news for you. We have another scroll for you that came up from the valley."

Nicholaus looked through the scrolls on his table and then reached over and picked up one from Levi's table. He unrolled the scroll and examined it before he handed it to Nicodemus.

Nicodemus thanked Nicholaus for the invitation to food and drink. He then went through his normal prayer ritual and helped himself to a goblet of wine. He then hurriedly opened the scroll and began to read.

Baptist III

From Judas Ben-Hakkatan, a Pharisee of Pharisees of the tribe of Judah and servant of the High Holy one of Israel, blessed is he, to the Council Ruling Elders in Jerusalem. Greetings and may the High Holy One of Israel, blessed is he, bless and keep you. Amen.

In obedience to your wish for us to observe and report on activities of the Baptist, the following observations, my second report, is hereby submitted for your approval.

A question arose with the Jews about purifying from John's disciples. And they came to John and said to him, "Teacher, the one who was with you beyond the Jordan, to whom you have witnessed, behold, this one baptizes, and all are coming to him."

John answered and said, "A man is able to receive nothing unless it has been given to him from heaven. You yourselves witnessed to me that I said I am not the Christ, but that having been sent, I am going before that One. The one having the bride is the bridegroom. But the friend of the bridegroom, standing and hearing him, rejoices with joy because of the bridegroom's voice. With this, my joy has been fulfilled. The One must increase, but I must decrease. The One coming from above is above all. The ones being of the earth is earthly and speaks of the earth. The one coming out of heaven is above all. And what he has seen and heard, this he testifies. And no one receives his testimony. The one receiving his testimony has sealed that God is true, for the one whom God sent speaks the words of God. For God does not give the Spirit by measure. The Father loves the Son and has given all things into his hand. The one believing into the Son has everlasting life, but the one disobeying the Son will not see life, but the wrath of God remains on him" (John 3:25–36) from the Greek.

The Lord bless you and keep you. The Lord make His face to shine upon you and be gracious to you. The Lord lift up his countenance upon you and give you peace. (Num. 6:24–26 from the Hebrew).

Nicodemus rolls up the scroll and quietly, in long contemplation, considered its contents. He then said, "The One coming from above is above all? Everlasting life? The wrath of God? I don't understand this man, this Son of the Father."

"Neither do I, but I am satisfied that this 'Son of the Father' and the 'sandal man' are one in the same person."

Nicodemus then shared that the council was interested in this sandal man and had sent people down to the Jordan Valley to find him. He was nowhere to be found, and speculation is that he may have gone up to Galilee. He then hurried off to the Council Chamber.

*****

Later, Levi approached the table with a man dressed as a Pharisee and introduced him as Ahikar Bar-Jathan from Cana of Galilee. It seemed that Levi had heard the man asking for the mediator Ben-Adon and introduced himself as Ben-Adon's apprentice and then took him to his table.

Nicholaus stood up and introduced himself to the man and asked him to join them.

The man said that he had just come down from Cana and that he had a scroll for the mediator Ben-Adon. The man produced the scroll from his robe and handed it across the table. Nicholaus took the scroll, looked at it for a moment, and then gave it to Levi. He paid the man five silver denarii and asked the man for the latest news from Cana.

"I have come down in response to the request from the Council in Sepphoris to forward information about Jesus of Nazareth. I first became aware of the Nazarene when I attended a wedding. It seems that the bridegroom had withheld the best wine to be served last. Some of the servants reported that, under his mother's orders, the Nazarene had caused them to fill the water pots with water and then serve it to the governor of the feast. As they served it to the governor, it was turned into new wine, but I didn't give much credit to their report" (John 2:1–11, from the Greek). Other than this, I don't have anything else to tell you."

The men then shared the pleasantries of the day, and after a time, Bar-Jathan excused himself and departed.

*****

Later that afternoon, a young man approached, asking if Nicholaus was Ben-Adon.

Nicholaus rose and said, "Yes, I am Awnee Ben-Adon."

The young man handed Nicholaus a scroll and said, "I'm sorry, sir, but I'm in a terrible hurry. May I please have my master's money?"

Nicholaus unrolled the scroll and saw that it was written in Hebrew and that it was from a Pharisee in the valley and that it was a report about the Baptist. With that, he rolled up the scroll and paid the young man.

The young man then scurried out of the building, without any other explanation.

A Ring

Levi and Eglah were on their usual morning meander through the marketplace, and they stopped at the shop of Jada Ben-Lahad. He wanted to look at bangles*.

A man and two ladies came into the shop. One of the ladies, Sarah, came running up to Levi and gave him a hug. "How long has it been? I haven't seen you in ages. Let me introduce you." Gesturing to the other lady, she said, "This is Haggith, my mistress, and this tall handsome gentleman is Malchus, our escort." She then introduced Levi. "And this is Levi, the mediator, my childhood friend. We grew up together right here in Jerusalem."

Levi then introduced Eglah to the group and then engaged himself in a conversation with Sarah, his long-lost friend.

Eglah and Haggith engaged in conversation as Malchus looked on and chatted with Ben-Lahad.

Haggith then made a small purchase, and the girl talk continued. After a while, the conversation was over, and Haggith, Sarah and Malchus said their good-byes and left the shop.

Levi then picked out a bangle and purchased it for Eglah. As they were getting ready to leave, Jada asked Levi if he knew who those people were.

"I only knew Sarah. I have no idea who the other two are."

"Haggith is the daughter of Caiaphas, the high priest, and Malchus is his servant. You were in the presence of priestly royalty."

Eglah was taken aback by this revelation and said, "I'm glad she didn't know anything about me."

*****

Meanwhile, Nicodemus arrived at Beth Eden and seated himself across from Nicholaus. They exchanged pleasantries, and Nicodemus helped himself to some bread and cheese. "The warmth of the sun felt awfully good on my poor tired old body today."

Nicholaus chuckled and nodded his understanding.

With that, Nicodemus asked, "Do you have anything for me today?"

"Yes." He handed him two new scrolls.

Galilean I

Greetings in the name of the High Holy One of Israel. May He give you peace.

In response to the request of the elders in Sepphoris, I, Judah Bar-Ohel, am sending you this report.

There is a new self-proclaimed prophet here in Nazareth. He presented himself in the synagogue and stood up to read. And the book of Isaiah the prophet was handed to him. And unrolling the scroll, he found the place where it was written, "The spirit of the Lord is upon me. Therefore He anoints me to preach the gospel to the poor. He has sent me to heal the broken-hearted, to preach deliverance to captives, and to give new sight to the blind, to send away crushed ones in deliverance, to preach an acceptable year of the Lord." (Isa. 61:1–2a from the Hebrew).

Returning the scroll to the attendant he sat down. The eyes of all in the synagogue were fixed on him, and he said to them, "Today this Scripture has been fulfilled in your ears."

And all bore witness to him and marveled at the words coming out of his mouth. And they said one to another, "Is this not the son of Joseph?"

And he said to them: "Surely you will speak this parable to me Physician heal yourself! What other we have heard done in Capernaum do also here in your country." But he said, "Truly I say to you that no prophet acceptable in his native place. Truly I say to you, there were many widows in Israel in the days of Elijah when the heavens were shut over three years and six months, and a great famine came on all the land, yet Elijah was sent to none of except to Zarephath of Siden to a widow woman. And many lepers were in Israel during the time of Elisha the prophet and none of them were made clean except Naaman, the Syrian."

All the people were filled with anger hearing these things in the synagogue. And rushing up, they threw him outside the city and led him up to the bow of the hill on which their city was built in order to throw him down, but he walked away passing through the midst, and we do not know where he is [Luke 4:16–30 from the Greek].

The Lord bless you and keep you. The Lord make His face to shine upon you and be gracious to you. The Lord lift up his countenance upon you and give you peace (Num. 6:24–26 from the Hebrew).

Nicodemus set the scroll aside. "This Nazarene must think himself to be a prophet and maybe even the Messiah."

Nicholaus nodded in agreement.

"And he walked away passing through the midst. How could he do that? Did he change his appearance or maybe he blinded their eyes or became invisible. How did he do it?"

"I don't know but apparently he did."

Galilean II

To the Council of Ruling Elders in Jerusalem, greetings and may the High Holy One of Israel, blessed is he, bless and keep you. Amen.

I, Ahikar Bar-Jathan, from Cana of Galilee, am forwarding this report of my observations as requested by the council in Sepphoris.

A nobleman from Capernaum came to Cana seeking the Nazarene, and when he found him, he asked him that he would come and heal his son for he was about to die.

Then the Nazarene said to him, "Unless you see signs and wonders you will not at all believe."

The nobleman said to him, "Sir, come down before my child dies."

The Nazarene said to him. "Go! Your son lives." And the man believed the word which Jesus said to him and went his way. [John 4:46–50 from the Greek]

It was later reported to us by Nathanael Bar-Tholomew, a follower of the Nazarene, that the son's fever left him that very same hour.

I have nothing further to report at this time.

The Lord bless you and keep you. The Lord make His face to shine upon you and be gracious to you. The Lord lift up his countenance upon you and give you peace. (Num. 6:24–26 from the Hebrew)

Nicodemus rolled up the scroll and added it to the other one. "He healed from Cana to Capernaum without having to go there. The council is going to be interested in this one.

Nicholaus nodded in agreement and then remarked that the healing was done on the father's faith in the word of the prophet.

"And what about this Nathanael Bar-Tholomew, one of his followers? Is he going to become one of our contributors?"

"Yes. That may be worth exploring." With that Nicodemus paid for the scrolls and departed for the council chambers.

Jada Ben-Lahad came in just as Nicodemus was leaving. They greeted each other as Jada was a Neeman, worthy of a greeting. Jada then went directly to Levi's table and gave him a list of contracts that he needed. "I am still very impressed with Eglah," he said. "And you need to know that when I held her hand, putting on the bangle, I calculated her ring size."

"Ring size? Aren't you getting a little bit ahead of yourself?" Levi questioned.

"Not at all. After all, remember, it hadn't rained yet when Noah built the ark." After a brief time of pleasantries, Jada excused himself and left.

*****

Later that day, Eglah had a sheepish grin on her face when she came up to Nicholaus's table. "We need to talk… if you don't mind taking the time to talk with me."

Nicholaus looked up and grinned. "Of course not, I always have time for a beautiful girl like you. Please, be seated and tell me what's on your mind."

Eglah sat down, patted Lady's head, and scratched her behind her ears. "I have two things on my mind that I need to talk to you about. First off, I'd like to thank you for sending Levi to escort me in the market. It is such a comfort to know that I have a protector."

Nicholaus assured her that it was his pleasure to know that she was properly being escorted.

Eglah then went on to say, "I have also been asked to invite you to a midday meal with my Mistress, Abishag, one week from today. She would like you to break bread with her up on the second floor. She has made arrangements for the meal and accommodations so that, as she puts it, you can get acquainted. Please do not follow the usual custom of denying for unworthiness. She says if anyone is unworthy, it is her."

Nicholaus was somewhat surprised at the invitation but assured Eglah that he would be there. Nicholaus wondered, *Now what does she want? It's not a request to write a new contract. She would have sent that down with Eglah. I'm sure it's not 'business' at my age. She knows better. I doubt it's to mediate a contract. She hasn't needed to do that in years. What can it be?*

Contracts

The young Hakkatan, a Levite and servant of Abner, made his way to the table of Nicholaus. Lady got up and went to his side to say hello. He patted her head and scratched behind her ears. "I know dogs are not popular here in Jerusalem, but I like them anyway. Their love is unconditional, and you can't help but like them." Lady wagged all over and then returned to her perch behind Nicholaus.

Nicholaus smiled in agreement as he greeted his friend. He offered him food and drink and asked him what he could do for him.

Hakkatan explained that Abner had sent him in place of Ben-Gorion. It seemed that he was otherwise occupied and unable to keep his weekly meeting. Hakkatan then asked if Nicholaus had any scrolls for the council.

Nicholaus replied that he had one scroll that had come down from Galilee and began going through his scrolls to find it.

Hakkatan then asked Nicholaus, "Master, why do people have a need for contracts when they know each other?"

Nicholaus replied, "Contracts are necessary to prevent people from having misunderstandings. People can be forgetful at times. Society would fall apart without contracts, my young friend. Contracts keep commerce moving, and they keep honest people honest and counteract forgetfulness."

Nicholaus then found the scroll he was looking for and handed it to Hakkatan.

Hakkatan took the scroll without looking at it and asked Nicholaus if he had any messages for the council.

Nicholaus assured him that he did not.

Hakkatan then thanked Nicholaus for his time and gave him a sealed pouch for the scroll he was given. He then excused himself and departed for the council chambers. Upon arriving at the council chambers, Hakkatan gave the scroll and unused sealed pouches to Abner. Ben-Gamaliel entered the office as Hakkatan was excusing himself to go about his other duties.

Abner and Ben-Gamaliel greeted each other as Pharisees, and then they had their morning rituals and prayer. Finally they helped themselves to the food and drink that had been prepared for them.

Abner gave the scroll marked "Galilean III" to Ben-Gamaliel, and he began to read it out loud.

Galilean III

Blessings to you from the High Holy One of Israel.

Greetings in the name of the High Holy One of Israel. May He give you peace.

I, Chelub Bar-Abihail, of the tribe of Levi, a Pharisee of Pharisees, declare that this is a true record of an event I witnessed.

A teacher from Nazareth stood up in the synagogue in Capernaum and was teaching. There was a man there who had the spirit of an unclean demon, and he cried out with a loud voice saying: "Ah! What have we to do with you, Jesus of Nazareth? Did you come to destroy us? I know you. You are the Holy one of God."

Jesus rebuked him. "Be silent and come out of him." And throwing the man into the midst, the demon came out from him, not harming him.

Astonishment came on us all and we spoke with one another saying what is this that he commands the unclean spirits with authority and power, and they came out? [Luke 4:31–36 from the Greek]

Another time, large crowds were coming to hear and to be healed from their infirmities by this same Jesus, and it happened that on one of these days when he was teaching, a man came carrying a man on a cot who was paralyzed, and they sought to bring him in and to lay him before him. But they could not find a way through which they might bring him through the crowd.

Going up on the rooftop, they let him down through the tiles with the cot into the midst of Jesus.

And seeing their faith, he said to him, "Man, your sins have been forgiven you."

And we began to reason, "Who is this who speaks blasphemy? Who is able to forgive sins except God alone?"

Then he said to us, "Why do you reason in your hearts? Which is easier, to say, your sins have been forgiven you or to say, rise up and walk. But that you might know that the son of man has authority on the earth to forgive sins."

He said to the paralytic, "I say to you rise up and take your cot and go to your house."

And rising up at once before us, the man took up that which he was laying on and went to his house glorifying God. [Luke 5:17–25 from the Greek]

These things I reported to the elders in Sepphoris, and upon their request, I am now forwarding this report to you.

The Lord bless you and keep you. The Lord make His face to shine upon you and be gracious to you. The Lord lift up his countenance upon you and give you peace. [Num. 6:24–26 from the Hebrew]

Ben-Gamaliel set the scroll aside and looked at Abner in astonishment. "The Holy One of God? Authority to forgive sins? Either this Jesus is a prophet sent from God or a sorcerer. I can't help but think there's more to be added to his ministry."

*****

At the appointed time, Nicholaus, staff in hand, made his way to the second floor for his rendezvous with Madam Abishag. Hamutal, a servant girl, was waiting for him at the head of the stairs and ushered him into a cubicle that had been prepared for them. Abishag was seated at one end of a table prepared for their luncheon. She got up for the appropriate greetings. Nicholaus then seated himself at the other end of the table.

Abishag began the conversation by thanking Nicholaus for joining her and saying that this is something they should have done a long time ago. She then thanked him for the kindness he had shown her in the writing and mediating of contracts for her and for providing an escort for Eglah.

Nicholaus assured her that he was happy to be of service, and he was in full agreement with Levi escorting Eglah to the market. "These days, it's just not safe for a girl to be in the market unescorted."

As the luncheon progressed and pleasantries were exchanged, Abishag brought up the subject of the developing relationship between Eglah and Levi. She then suggested that they should consider a marriage between the two. She went on to say that Eglah has no family so there was no one to engage a matchmaker.

Nicholaus considered the question for a moment and then replied that Levi also did not have a family to engage a matchmaker. The fact was that he and Levi were the only family either one of them had. He then suggested that it might be appropriate for him and Abishag to make the necessary arrangements. "We are born into a certain time and place, and there is nothing we can do to control it."

Abishag agreed and suggested that if the couple were in agreement, a betrothal should be arranged as soon as possible.

Nicholaus agreed and said that he would discuss the matter with Levi and let her know what the answer was going to be.

The luncheon continued as the two continued getting acquainted and exchanging pleasantries.

After the luncheon was over, Nicholaus sought out Levi to discuss the situation with him. Nicholaus was not surprised that Levi was very excited about the possibility and started making the necessary arrangements for his participation in a betrothal.

15

The Tax Collector

Nicholaus and Nicodemus enjoyed their early morning meal together. Nicodemus asked about Levi and was assured that Levi and Eglah were at the market. Eventually, after the meal, Nicodemus got down to business. "Do you have anything for me to today?"

Nicholaus sorted out a scroll and then hands it to Nicodemus. "Yes, I have just one. I think you will find it interesting."

Galilean IV

I, Simon Bar-Gaal, the Pharisees of Pharisees and teacher of teachers, here in Capernaum, have become aware of the activities of a false prophet, one Jesus of Nazareth.

A tax collector named Levi had a great feast for this false prophet in his home. There was a crowd of many tax collectors reclining and others who were with them. And we asked his disciples why he eats and drinks with tax collectors and sinners.

And he answered, "Those who are sound have no need for a physician but those who have sickness. I did not come to call the righteous to

repentance but sinners" [Matt. 9:9–13, Mark
2:13–14 from the Greek].

He paused and thought for a moment, and then he questioned,
"Sin is a sickness? Is the sickness sin? Nicodemus then goes back to
reading the scroll.

> Then we asked him, "Why do John's disciples fast
> often and make prayers and likewise those of the
> Pharisees, but those close to you eat and drink?"

He answered saying, "You are not able to make the sons of the
bride chamber* fast while the bridegroom is with them. But days will
come when the bridegroom is taken away from them, then in those
days they will fast." He then told us some story about old garments
and wineskin that was totally ridiculous. [Matt. 9:10–12, Mark
2:15–17, and Luke 5:27–38 from the Greek]

> This Nazarene is clearly a false prophet, and he
> needs to be dealt with.

Nicodemus rolled up the scroll and paused for a moment. Then
he said, "I think this Bar-Gaal is rather quick to form an opinion,
with very little investigation. I'd much rather he reports the facts and
keep his opinions to himself."

Nicholaus smiled and said, "I am inclined to agree with your
assessment of Bar-Gaal. Also, the comment Jesus made about the
bridegroom reminded me of the "friend of the bridegroom" comment made by the Baptist earlier."

With this, Nicodemus left Beth Eden and headed for the council chambers.

*****

Later that morning, Rhodocus Ben-Merari and his entourage
came in and went directly to Levi's table. "We have some contracts

for you to write, and we expect you to drop everything else and do them right away," he exclaimed with an attitude of authority.

Lady jumped up and growled, the fur on her back standing up. Nicholaus grabbed her under her belly and his left hand over her snout.

Levi paused for a moment and gathered his wits about him. Instead of rising like he normally would, he remained seated. He looked up at Ben- Keziath with a smile on his face and said, "I am sorry, sir, but I do not operate that way. You will have to wait your turn, just like everyone else does. Your contracts will be ready for you sometime next week, and I suggest that if that's not satisfactory, you take your request somewhere else. I have work to do, and I cannot be bothered with requests that are out of order." With that, Ben-Merari and his entourage turned and left, heading for another table.

Nicholaus had a big smile on his face as he congratulated Levi in the way he conducted himself before one of Jerusalem's notorious despots.

"It would be really easy to get to hate that man," Levi exclaimed.

"Don't do that. Pity him. The only person that is affected by hate is the person doing the hating. The people you hate don't know it, and the rest just don't care."

*****

At the appointed time, Nicholaus and Levi ascended to their second-floor rendezvous. Nicholaus had his staff in hand, and Lady led the way. She headed straight for the kitchen as soon as she hit the top of the stairs. Levi followed and was obviously very nervous. He had prepared himself for the meeting by putting on his finest robe and anointing himself with a pleasant fragrance. He had the ketubah* rolled up in his hand, a beautifully decorated formal document that specified the marriage terms and stated his intent to consecrate himself to his bride to be.

The young serving girl, Hamutal, had a big smile on her face as she waited for them at the top of the stairs. She then led them to a cubicle where Abishag and Eglah are seated at the low table. The table is set with a fine meal for four. The women stood and greeted. Nicholaus and Abishag took their places at the ends of the table, right and left. Levi sat himself with his back to the Veil. Eglah pours wine for the three of them but left the cup in front of her empty. She then took her seat.

Levi stood and described his few but growing assets. His skills as a mediator were also growing. He could read and write in Hebrew, Aramaic, Greek, Latin, and a few other lesser languages. His devotion for Eglah is undivided, and he now stated, "I will betroth you to me forever. Yes, I will betroth you to me in righteousness and in judgment and in mercy and, in compassion. I will even betroth you to me in faithfulness [Hosea 2:19–20a from the Hebrew]. I am now asking that you be my wife." He then sat himself.

At this point, all attention was on Eglah. She remained seated with her head bowed in apparent contemplation. She then stood and reached for the wineskin and poured some wine into her cup. She sat and took a sip, signifying her acceptance of the proposal.

Levi presented the ketubah and stated his intent to consecrate himself to his bride to be. He then stood up and declared, "Behold, thou art Betrothed unto me, with this ring, in accordance with the Law of Moses and Israel." He then placed a gold ring on her ring finger, symbolizing his eternal commitment. Next he poured another cup of wine and offered it to Eglah. She took the cup and drank of it, indicating the covenant is sealed and they are betrothed. Eglah now lifted the head scarf from her shoulders up over her head to cover her hair. From this point on, she would always wear her shawl, or a head scarf, over her hair in public to indicate her status as a married woman.

The ketubah is now signed and dated by all present as bride, bridegroom, and witnesses. All four joined hands, and Nicholaus offered a prayer: "Splendor is upon everything. Blessing is upon everything. You are Holy, Adonai, in your presence permeates the universe through your commandments. We share your holiness. You teach us to rejoice with the bride and groom, to celebrate their consecration to each other, to witness their vows to each other. Blessings, happiness, long life, and prosperity we pray for this young couple."

The veil on the cubicle is now pushed aside, and the four come out.

There are no secrets in Beth Eden. The four are greeted by a gathering of merchants from the first floor and ladies from the third floor rejoicing together in the betrothal of their friends. Even the Romans came up to join in the festivities and offer their congratulations.

*****

Two days later, there was another gathering on the second floor. This included Nicholaus, Abishag, and the centurion Manlius. Manlius has developed an affection for Levi as a writer of contracts. He was determined that he and his men must have some part in the wedding. Also present were the sisters Mary and Joann.

Abishag suggested that the first thing they must discuss is the wedding ceremony and where the wedding could be held.

Manlius suggested holding it in the Roman room. Nicholaus said that he thought that might work. The sisters said that they would help with the set-up and arrangements.

Abishag then asked, "What about the wedding feast? Where can we hold the wedding feast?"

Nicholaus then said, "Why not hold it right here on the second floor. That way, everything would be right here in Beth Eden

Manlius said, "My cooks can help with the preparations, and my troops can gather together provisions from the outlying communities. We need Merab, the head cook."

Mary got up and headed for the second-floor kitchen to get Merab.

Nicholaus then questioned, "Where are they going to live?"

Abishag said, "I have a place just north and east of here that was surrendered to me in place of compensation for services rendered. It is unoccupied and small, but it would be just right for them to get started.

Manlius then said, "Let us know how much you want for it, and the Roman band will pay for it." Looking at Nicholaus, he said, You and Levi have saved us lots of money over the years. This is the least we can do to repay your kindness.

"That sounds acceptable. The only thing we have left to do now is attend to the details and set a date for the wedding."

Nicholaus suggested the first of next month. Sooner is better than later to prevent interference by outsiders.

Mary returned with Merab, the head cook and manager of the second-floor kitchen. Merab declared, "I understand you are planning a wedding. It's about time. Those two have been falling all over each other for weeks now. What's the plan?"

After much more discussion about the finer details, everyone was satisfied that all the arrangements have been made, and the wedding will be held on the first of the following month.

16

The Wedding Day

Eglah tossed and turned all night trying to get some sleep. She just couldn't quit thinking about her wedding day tomorrow and her wedding night. *Will he consider my body attractive? Will I be good enough? Will it hurt? Will I please him?* The ladies had set her down and had a long conversation with her, and they answered all her questions. But she was still apprehensive. And what about everything that occurred to make it happen? She was the luckiest girl in all of Israel. She knew that she wanted to marry Levi the first time she saw him, and now it was going to happen. She had not been hampered by the interference of a matchmaker, and Mistress Abishag had finally made it happen. Eventually, with all the questions in her mind, she had fallen asleep, and the next thing she knew, the ladies were getting her up.

This was a most exciting day for the ladies. This was as close as most of them would ever come to having a wedding of their own, and they intended to make the most of it. Today, Eglah was their queen, and they were going to make it a royal occasion. It started off with a bath in scented water, followed by the anointing, the dusting, and doing her hair. Her hair was not platted as theirs was; it was done up in the high-class fashion of royalty. She was then dressed with the finest white garments they had made especially for her. Pure white represented spiritual pureness.

The ladies then seated her on her bridal throne. They then danced around her, complementing her, calling her the most beautiful and gracious bride. They then took turns presenting her with her wedding gifts. These were her dowry, the rest of her trousseau, and everything she might need for the wedding, the wedding night, and her new life as a wife to Levi. They were all a part of her retinue*. They all loved Eglah and did everything they could to show it.

Finally, the cry is heard. "The bridegroom is coming! The bridegroom is coming! Make ready, the bridegroom is coming!"

Mistress Abishag escorted Eglah to the landing at the top of the stairs. All the ladies fell in behind her. Levi was escorted by Nicholaus and an entourage of Roman commanders in full ceremonial dress. Business and trading were halted for the day, and all the men of the first floor have assembled in the second-floor dining area and are cheering the entourage on.

When Nicholaus and Levi reached the third-floor landing, they gave formal greetings to Mistress Abishag and Eglah. They in turn returned formal greetings to Nicholaus and Levi. Levi then lifts Eglah's veil from the top of her head and lowers it over her face. This is reminiscent of Rebecca's covering her face with her veil upon seeing Isaac before their marriage. The covering of the face symbolizes the modesty, dignity, and chastity, which characterizes the virtues of Jewish womanhood.

Nicholaus and Abishag led the procession down the stairs, followed by Levi and Eglah, arm in arm. The ladies followed suite, singing and rejoicing as they went.

As the procession passed the second floor, all the men of the trading floor mingled with the ladies and joined in the singing and rejoicing. The Romans were gathered on the first floor, and they mingled in as the procession entered the Roman room.

When the procession reaches the Roman room, they are greeted by the sight of the chuppah*, the wedding canopy, in the center of the room. The chuppah is made of fine linen, about five cubits* square. Each corner was suspended from the shaft of a Roman spear being held by four Roman soldiers in full ceremonial uniforms.

When they approached the chuppah, all the knots on Levi's garments are untied. This symbolizes that at the moment of marriage, all other bonds were eliminated except the intimate one between the bride and groom.

The attendants then put a traditional white robe on Levi. This serves to remind the groom of the solemnity of the occasion.

Madam Abishag and Eglah now circle Levi seven times, representing a sevenfold bond, which marriage will establish between the bride and groom.

Nicodemus had been standing on the opposite side of the chuppah. He now spoke as loud as he could: "Welcome! He who is the Almighty, the Omnipotent overall, he who is blessed over all, he who is the greatest of all shall bless the bride and the groom." He then entered the chuppah, as do Levi and Eglah, along with Nicholaus and Madam Abishag.

An attendant hands Nicodemus, a goblet of wine. He in turn gives it to Levi, and both Levi and Eglah drink of it, symbolizing joy and abundance. The first blessing over the wine signifies the just; as we pronounce the Holiness of the Sabbath and festivals over the wine we sanctify the personal relationship of marriage.

Nicodemus now recites the seven wedding blessings. "1. Blessed are you, Jehovah, who brings forth fruit from the vine. 2. Blessed are you, Jehovah, who shapes the universe. All things created, speak of your glory. 3. Blessed are you, Holy One, who fashions each person. 4. We bless you, Jehovah, for forming each person in your image. You have planted with in us a vision of view and given us the measure that we may flourish through time, blessed are you, creator of humanity. 5. May Israel, once bereft of her children, now delight as they gather together in joy. Blessed are you, Jehovah, who lets the Zion rejoice with her children. 6. Let these loving friends taste of the blessing you gave to the first man and woman in the Garden of Eden in the days of old. Blessed are you, the presence who dwells with the bride and groom in delight. 7. Blessed are you who lights the world with happiness and contentment, love and companionship, peace and friendship, Bridegroom and Bride. Let the mountains of Israel, dance! Let the gates of Jerusalem ring with the sounds of joy, song, merriment, and delight, the voice of the groom and the voice of the bride, the happy shouts of their friends and companions. We bless you, Jehovah, who brings bride and groom together to rejoice in each other."

Levi then reads the Ketubah, the marriage contract. In essence he obligates himself to his Bride. He pledges to work for her, honor, and provide for and support her. He will strengthen and affirm his bride's dignified status. He will provide her with a home, feed her, cloth her and give her conjugal rights. "I promise to stand by you always, to be joy in your heart, and food to your soul. To bring out the best in you always, and for you, to be the most that I can be. To laugh with you in good times and struggle with you through life's challenges. May we strive to bring to fruition; both are shared in our individual hopes and dreams. Let us build our home on a foundation of trust, respect, and generosity of spirit, guided by the Torah's values and traditions. May our lives be embraced by peace and love. And when we grow old, may we walk together hand-in-hand, still feeling the sweetness of our devotion. I give myself without reservation to our union and welcome you as my partner in life. May our home and family be bestowed with blessings and peace."

Nicholaus then prayed his own special prayer for the young couple. The attendant then handed him a wine glass wrapped in a napkin. He in turn placed the glass on the floor in front of Levi's right foot. Levi stamps on the glass, breaking it, symbolizing man's short life on earth that even in the midst of a happy occasion, we should not forget how fragile life truly is. Nicodemus then declared that they are husband-and-wife.

With this, the guests shout, "Mazel tov," and clapped their hands.

Two Big Hands

Levi was in the Roman room, picking up some requests for contracts from the centurion Manlius. He mentioned that these were going to keep him busy, and he would be unable to escort Eglah to the market on the morrow.

Manlius said that he and his men were going to be in the market tomorrow morning, and he would keep an eye out for her.

Levi thanked him for his courtesies and excused himself to return to his work.

The following day, Eglah was making her usual rounds of the booths when a silken headscarf caught her eye. She stopped and out of curiosity asked the price.

The merchant was very abrupt with her and quoted her a most outlandish price.

Eglah was taken aback by both the man's attitude and in the quoted price. She then asked why the headscarf was so expensive.

The merchant, with a rough, nasty tone, answered that a scarf like that was too good for the likes of her, and besides, prices were always double for a third-floor whore.

With that, two big hands suddenly came from behind Eglah, reached across the table, grabbed the merchant by his cloak, and lifted him up into the air. "This is no whore!" came the deep loud voice of Manlius. "She is Eglah, the wife of Levi, the mediator, the man who writes contracts for you, and she is as pure as the water in the pool of Siloam. You are to treat her with the respect due a queen, and if you don't, I'm going to come back here and cut your balls off. Do you understand?

The man, pale with fright, nodded his head yes.

Manlius continued to hold the man up in the air and said, "I can't hear you! Do you understand?"

The man timidly said, "Yes."

Manlius still held the man even higher in the air and repeated himself: "I still can't hear you! Speak up, you stupid offspring of a drunken camel. Do you understand?"

The man then shouted, "Yes, I understand she is to be treated with the utmost respect."

Manlius then lowered the man to his seat and straightened out his cloak for him. Then he picked up the silken headscarf Eglah was looking at and handed it to her. Then he picked up two more silken headscarves and handed them to her also. "These are for you, my lady. They are a gift from this most grateful merchant."

With that, the merchant voiced his most humble apologies and full agreement of the gift. He was still bowing and shaking in his sandals as the two of them left his stall. Eglah had a big smile on her face as she walked down the road with a new silk scarf on her head and on the arm of a very tall and very strong Roman.

From that day on, Eglah always wore a silken headscarf when she went to the market, and she was treated with more and more respect as the story of her and the protection of her escort spread among the merchants.

*****

Nicodemus came in with a smile on his face. He seated himself across from Nicholaus and proceeded to help himself to some fruit and wine, without an invitation or the usual rituals of a Pharisee. A light-hearted conversation about the events of the week ensued with Nicholaus joining in with some bread and cheese, along with a mug of wine.

Lady returned from her morning travels and stopped by Nicodemus's side for her weekly pat on the head. She then curled up behind Nicholaus's chair.

Nicholaus picked up the conversation where they had left off; then he sat his mug aside and reached for a scroll. "I have another scroll for you. It's down from Capernaum." With that, he handed Nicodemus the scroll.

Nicodemus unrolled the scroll and began to read.

Galilean V

I am Chelub Bar-Abihail, the Levite of Capernaum. To the Council of Ruling Elders in Jerusalem, greetings and may the High Holy One of Israel, blessed is he, bless and keep you. Amen.

I am sending you this report at the request of the Ruling Council of Elders in Sepphoris. It was their judgment that this report was worthy of your consideration.

There is a publican here in Capernaum named Levi. And Levi made a great feast for Jesus of Nazareth in his home. And there was a crowd of many tax collectors reclining and of others who were with them.

Nicodemus lowered the scroll and looking across the table at Nicholaus with a questioning expression on his face. He then said, "I have read this scroll before."

Nicholaus just smiled and said, "No, you haven't. Keep reading, or you will miss the best part." Nicodemus picked up the scroll again found his place and continue to read.

And our scribes and the Pharisees that were with me asked his disciples, "Why do you eat and drink with tax collectors and sinners?" Jesus said to them, "Those who are sound have no need of a physician, but those who have sickness. I did not come to call the righteous to repentance, but sinners."

But they said to him, "Why do John's disciples fast often and make prayers and likewise those of the Pharisees, but those close to you eat and drink?"

"You are not able to make the sons of the bridegroom fast while the bridegroom is with them. But days will come when the bridegroom is taken away from them, then in those days they will fast."

And he also told a parable to them, "No one puts a piece of a new garment on an old garment; otherwise, both the new and the old will tear, and the old does not match the piece from the new. And no one puts new wine into old skins; otherwise, the new wine will burst the skins, and it will be poured out, and the skins will perish. But new wine is to be put into new skins, and both are preserved together. And no one drinking immediately desires new for he says, the old is better." [Luke 5:29–38 from the Greek]

I have nothing more to report at this time. The Lord bless you and keep you. The Lord make His face to shine upon you and be gracious to you. The Lord lift up his countenance upon you and give you peace. [Num. 6:24–26 from the Hebrew]

Nicodemus lowered the scroll to the table. "This reads like the report from Bar-Gaal." He paused in contemplation and then asked, "You can't mix the old with the new?"

Nicholaus replied, "Yes, and tell me, is he telling us that our temple worship is to be replaced by this new kingdom?"

Nicodemus pondered the question. "That is a very good question. I will have to take it up with the council." With that, Nicodemus paid Nicholaus his dues and hurried off to the council chambers.

Ben-Benjamin, who had the table just beyond Levi's, announced his retirement. This left his table open. Levi suggested strongly that they obtain the table and bring Bar-Ananiel up from the back row and make him a small part of their association. Nicholaus had been feeling the burden of more work, and old age was creeping up on him and quickly agreed provided that Bar-Ananiel was willing to join with them. The arrangements for the table were quickly made, and Levi hurried off to get his friend Daniel.

Nicholaus got up from his chair and welcomed Daniel to his new table. The three men sat down and had a leisure time of refreshment and getting better acquainted with each other.

Nicholaus then gave a lesson on procedures to Daniel. "First off, you must learn the current values of the items being contracted. Don't be afraid to ask one of us. Use the native language of people entering into the contract when you speak to them. If necessary, be a teacher and an interpreter for them. Remain neutral at all times. Prepare your mind for the work ahead. Stay alert. Be self-controlled, and remember that there are no friends or enemies in contract writing. Never violate the laws of Rome or the Laws of Moses. Always make three copies of every contract. One for each of the buyers in the language of the buyer, one in the language of the seller, and one in Greek for your records. Don't be rushed during negotiations. Take your time and double-check everything. Don't force it. If you reach an impasse, drop it. There will be no contract. Always underpromise and overdeliver everything, and remember, you will never make everyone happy. If everyone wants something more, then it's in the contract, you have done a good job."

After the time of light conversation, Bar-Ananiel said that there were no Pharisees in the Khabur Valley where he comes from. He then asked what they can tell him about them.

Nicholaus then explained that Pharisees are fervent believers in keeping the Law of Moses, the Written Law, and the Oral Law. Within Pharisee circles, it was taught that there were seven types Pharisees:

1.   The God-loving, one who obeys God out of true love and affection for him

2. The God-fearing, or timid, one who has great reverence and respect for God out of fear of punishment
3. The blind, one who avoids everything going on around him
4. The pestle or hump-backed, one who, like the blind, makes a show of his avoidance of temptation
5. The ever-reckoning, one who questions everything with indecisiveness
6. The wait-a-little-while, one who takes no action until the situation is resolved by someone else
7. The shoulder, one who advertises his good deeds for all to see

He went on to explain that most of the Pharisees in Jerusalem today are the descendants of Pharisees and that some of them have lost sight of the motivations of their heritage. Like most religious organizations, the objectives of the founders are soon lost to the ambitions and whims of their descendants. The Pharisees of today are not the Pharisees of a few generations ago. He then advised that when dealing with a Pharisee, he must remember to address them with utmost respect and to never say any of the names of God, say "the High Holy One of Israel."

"What about the Romans? At home, the rule was stay out of sight, and if you see one, run away."

"The Romans here are the Italian Band of the Tenth Fretensis Legion. They are commanded by Marcus Gaius Manlius, a centurion, who is a personal friend of mine. I was born a citizen of Rome, and I have a special relationship with them. We write all their contracts for them. You will find that they are peacekeepers that live and let live as long as there is no violation of Roman law and their tribute is being paid. Just watch how Master Levi deal with them, and you will be all right."

A light conversation continued for a while, and then Bar-Ananiel excused himself and returned to his table.

Touched a Leper

Fall had turned into winter, and Eglah, on the arm of her husband, had a large smile on her face as she made the rounds in the market. Baara and Cozbi were also with them for the first time. Their duties were growing along with their experience and responsibilities.

The merchants all gave them warm greetings and were eager to display their wares. The women all gathered around them with much to talk about the events of the day and giving her their congratulations. Eglah was "Showing!"

*****

Nicodemus hurried along on his weekly trip to Beth Eden. There was a chill in the air and an occasional flake of snow. He pulled his cloak up tight around him; he just didn't like the cold, and the snow added to his displeasure. Snow belongs on Mount Eohron, not in Jerusalem. He was happy to feel the warmth of Beth Eden and determined that he was in no big hurry to leave. Reaching Nicholaus's table, he removed his cloak and hung it over the back of the chair. He then removed a special gift for his friend Lady. It was a camel's blanket that he carefully folded and placed behind Nicholaus's chair for Lady to curl up on. He then seated himself and reached for some bread and cheese.

Nicholaus thanked him in behalf of Lady and then joined him in their weekly morning meal together and the events of the week became the subject of conversation. He then introduced him to Daniel, and the small talk continued among the three.

Nicholaus eventually declared that he had a scroll from Cana for the council. He then handed a scroll to Nicodemus.

Nicodemus unrolled the scroll and began to read.

Galilean VI

To the Council of Ruling Elders in Jerusalem, greetings and may the High Holy One of Israel, blessed is he, bless and keep you. Amen.

I, Ahikar Bar-Jathan, from Cana of Galilee, am forwarding this report of a story as it was given to me by Nathanael Bar-Tholomew.

He was with Jesus when great crowds were following him. And behold coming up, a leper worshiped him, saying, "Lord, if you will, you are able to cleanse me."

And stretching out his hand, Jesus touched him, saying, "I will. Be cleansed!"

Nicodemus lowered the scroll and looked at Nicholaus. "He touched him. He actually reached out and touched a leper? I just can't understand this man." He then picked up the scroll, found where he left off, and continues to read.

And instantly his leprosy* was cleansed.

And Jesus said to him, "See that you tell no one, but go, show yourself to the Priest, and offer the gift which Moses commanded, for a testimony to them. [Matt. 8:2–4 from the Greek]

I have nothing further to report at this time.

The Lord bless you and keep you. The Lord make His face to shine upon you and be gracious to you. The Lord lift up his countenance upon

you and give you peace. [Num. 6:24–26 from the Hebrew]

Nicodemus rolled up the scroll and looked across the table at Nicholaus. "I just can't believe it. He reached out and touched a leper and cleansed him of his leprosy. What will he think of next?"

Nicholaus then said that he was reminded of a passage in Isaiah. "Say to those of a hasty heart, be strong! Your God will come with vengeance with the full dealing of God; he will come and save you. Then the eyes of the blind shall be opened. The lame shall leap like a deer, and the tongue of the dumb shall sing" (Isa. 35:4 from the Hebrew).

With that, Nicodemus took another mug of wine and some bread and cheese. Small talk continued for a while, and then Nicodemus excused himself, bundled up, and hurried off to the council chambers.

After Nicodemus left, a young man of a tall and broad stature, entered Beth Eden approached the table where Nicholaus was seated. "I am seeking the mediator Awnee Ben-Adon, and by the description I was given, you must be him."

Nicholaus arose and greeted the young man. He asked him to take a seat and offered him food and drink.

The young man seated himself and offered Nicholaus a scroll. "My name is Simon Ben-Cleopas, and I am the indentured servant of Simon Bar-Gaal of Capernaum. My instructions were to deliver these two scrolls to you and return ten silver denarii to my master."

Nicholaus looked at the scrolls and recognized that it was written in near-perfect Hebrew. He rolled them up and placed it on the table along with some other scrolls. He paid the man, and again he offered him food and drink, and this time he timidly took a fig. Nicholaus then said, "Tell me, my friend, what's the news from Capernaum?"

The young man paused for a moment and then replied, "The big thing right now is the completion of the new synagogue that was built for us by a Roman centurion. It is a magnificent structure, the largest building in the whole city, and we are anxious to start worshiping there."

The two continued with their small talk until the young man had finished eating his fig and had a mug of wine. He then excused himself, took his money, and departed.

*****

Later that afternoon, Malchus, the servant of Caiaphas, came in with some request for contracts to give to Levi and Daniel.

They joined Nicholaus at his table for a time of conversation and refreshment. Nicholaus asked Malchus about the latest news from the Council of Fourteen.

Malchus said that they were all concerned about the arrangements for Passover. It seems that Caiaphas and his followers did not want to bring the moneychangers and merchants into the Court of the Gentiles as they have in years past. "The Planning Committee has determined that they had to. There was nowhere else to put them. Caiaphas said that he did not want another incident with the Nazarene or his followers like they had last year. Last year's incident had cost them thousands of thousands* of silver shekels, and they just can't afford to do that again. The committee would just have to make room somewhere else outside the temple. The discussion then centered on clearing out the upper market or using the theater or the hippodrome. This has gone on and on for days, and there's still no end in sight."

Nicholaus said, "We have no indication that the Nazarene has been in Jerusalem since the Passover last year. There is always the possibility that he will not be here this year."

The group pondered this possibility and continued with their light conversation and time of refreshment.

*****

That evening on the roof with Hantili, Sheva, and Chilion, the conversation came around to Bar-Shual. Sheva said, "He had come into the shop and said that he wanted to order money pots, as many as we can make. He signed the contracts with no trouble and didn't haggle over the price. He was just as nice as he could be."

Nicholaus nodded that he understood but wondered if there would be a problem when it came time to collect.

Chilion then reported that for the last few weeks, he has been in the market collecting alms, and someone has been kicking him as they went by. His friend Jacob has started watching to see who is doing it, and he said that it was Rhodocus Ben-Keziath and his followers.

Nicholaus said that he would speak to his friends about this, and maybe they could do something about it.

The conversation then turned to lighter things and the events of the day. As darkness fell, the men retired for the evening.

19

More Bother Than He's Worth

Nicodemus was just entering Beth Eden when Sheva pushed past him and ran up to Nicholaus's table.

"Excuse me, Master, Bar-Shual just came back to my shop, and he brought a whole squad of temple guards with him. They took all of the money pots that I had made and only paid me half of the price agreed on. I told him we had a contract, but he said that he did not recognize contracts written by Greeks. He and the guards then left the shop with all my pots and only left half the money that was due.

Nicodemus had walked up behind them and heard Sheva's story.

Nicholaus said, "Excuse me for a minute. Wait here, and I will be right back."

Nicodemus introduced himself to Sheva and asked what had happened. Sheva explained how Bar-Shual had come to his shop inquiring about money pots. He had told Nicholaus about it. Nicholaus had written some contracts for both of them to sign. Now Bar-Shual refused to honor the contracts and walked off with all his pots and paid only half of what was due.

Nicholaus returned and gave Sheva a pouch. Nicholaus said, "This is the rest of the money that was due you. Leave your copy of the contract here with me, and I will take care of it."

Sheva gave Nicholaus a hug and a kiss on each cheek, thanking him profusely. He then excused himself and left.

Nicodemus seated himself without the normal greetings. "If you like, I can take care of this for you. I know Ben-Caiaphas and I have had dealings with Bar-Shual before. I should have no problem collecting the rest of what is due."

Nicholaus gave the contract to Nicodemus and thanked him for intervening. He went on to say that he knew there was going to be a problem with Bar-Shual, and he was glad that Sheva had come to him before Bar-Shual placed an order. There are some people that just shouldn't have the positions that they have, even though they were qualified when they first got the job.

Nicodemus agreed and said that if it was up to him, Bar-Shual would have been discharged years ago. He then asked if there were any new scrolls for him.

Nicholaus then handed Nicodemus two scrolls and said, "Here are some more down from Capernaum."

Nicodemus unrolled the first scroll and began to read.

Galilean VII

I, Simon Bar-Gaal, the Pharisee of Pharisees and teacher of teachers, here in Capernaum, have become aware of future activities of the false prophet, Jesus of Nazareth.

On the second Chief Sabbath*, we saw the false prophet passed along through the sown fields. And his disciples plucked the heads and were eating, rubbing with their hands. And we said to them, "Why do you do that which is not lawful to do on the Sabbath?"

He then said to us, "Have you never read what David did when he had need and hungered, he and those with him, how he entered the House of God in the days of Abiathar, the high priest, and did eat of the showbread, which was not lawful to eat except for the priest and he

even gave to those being with him? The Sabbath
came into being for man's sake, not man for the
Sabbath's sake. So then the Son of Man is Lord of
the Sabbath also." [Matt. 12:1–8, Mark 2:23–28,
and Luke 6:1–5 from the Greek]

Strong measures must be taken to silence
this false prophet.

Nicodemus rolled up the scroll and placed it in his robe.
And then he declared, "Plucking heads and rubbing them in your
hands is harvesting and thrashing. That is a clear violation of the
Sabbath."

Nicholaus then said, "Is not gleaning an accepted practice? And
is it wrong to satisfy one's hunger without trying to turn a profit?"

Nicodemus then unrolled the second scroll and begin to read.

Galilean VIII

I, Simon Bar-Gaal, the Pharisee of Pharisees
and teacher of Pharisees, here in Capernaum,
have become aware of another incident involving
the false prophet.

Nicodemus lowered the scroll and asked, "Why did he send two
scrolls when he could've put them both on one?" He then continued
to read.

The false prophet was in the synagogue, and there
was a man who had a withered hand. And we
watched him if he will heal him on the Sabbath
that we might accuse him.

He said to the man who had the withered
hand, "Rise up into the middle." Then he said to
us, "Is it lawful to do good on the Sabbath or to
do evil? To save the soul or to kill?"

We all remained silent.

He then said to the man, "Stretch out your hand!" And he stretched out, and his hand was restored, sound as the other.

We then went out and counseled with the Herodians* against him as to how we might destroy him. [Matt. 12:9–14, Mark 3:1–6, and Luke 6:6–11 from the Greek]

Nicodemus lowered the scroll and, looking at Nicholaus, said, "They went to the Herodians without checking with the council first! This Bar-Gaal is an idiot. He is letting his emotions get the better of him. He's going to end up being more bother than he's worth."

"I have another situation that we need to discuss," Nicholaus stated. "But first, I need to send Levi into the Roman room." Turning to Levi, he said, "Please go to the Roman room and see if the centurion Manlius is there, and if he is, asked him to join us."

Levi soon returned with the centurion. The two men got up and gave him greetings.

Nicholaus then got right down to business. "You remember the sisters Mary and Joann that worked with us putting together Eglah's wedding. Well, Mary has a son who is blind, and he gleans alms in the market. Lately, every time Rhodocus Ben-Keziath or one of his followers goes past him, they kick him. Being blind, he never sees it coming, and he cannot defend himself. I would consider it a most kind favor if something could be done about this." Each of the men agreed that this was wrong, and they would do whatever they could to stop it. With that the Manlius excused himself and returned to the Roman room.

Nicholaus and Nicodemus relaxed and continued with their discussions and had a leisurely time together.

Just as Nicodemus was getting ready to leave, Ahikar Bar-Jathan from Cana came in. The two men got up and greeted him, and then all three of them sat down

Lady lifted up her head from her camel's blanket, sniffed the air, and lay back down.

Nicholaus invited Bar-Jathan to help himself to food and drink. Bar-Jathan timidly took a fig and then asked if their sandal man project had gleaned any results.

Nicodemus replied, "Well, first off, we are satisfied that the sandal man is Jesus of Nazareth. He thinks the spirit of the Lord is upon him, and he has been anointed to preach the gospel, as predicted in Isaiah. You reported that when in Cana, he healed the son of a nobleman who was in Capernaum. Since then, he has healed a demon-possessed man on the Sabbath and a paralyzed man, forgiving his sins. He has feasted with tax collectors and sinners and considers himself a physician to sinners. The last report we had was that he healed a leper by reaching out and touching him. There just seems to be no end to the things this man does."

Bar-Jathan then said, "There is some talk in Cana about this Jesus being the Messiah. Is there any indication that he is a descendent of King David or that he has done anything to free Israel from Roman occupation?

Nicholaus replied that there are no indications of either.

"Well, the Nazarene has been in Jerusalem. We have a report from Nathaniel Bar-Tholomew of a healing at the pool of Bethesda. It's all recorded here in the scroll." He then handed a scroll to Nicholaus. Nicholaus handed the scroll to Levi, and a casual conversation of current events continued among the three men.

*****

That afternoon Rhodocus Ben-Merari and his entourage came storming into Beth Eden, and up to Nicholaus's table.

Levi reached down and grabbed Lady up into his lap, holding her tightly, as she growled her disapproval. Daniel looked up with a startled expression on his face.

Ben-Merari, glaring at Nicholaus, declared, "You cheated my friend Ben-Resheph. You wrote a contract between him and Bar-Keziath, the oil merchant, and he charged Ben-Resheph too much. Bar-Keziath now refuses to give him his oil at a fair price. You are the mediator. You must force Bar-Keziath to give up his oil."

Nicholaus kept his cool and just looked across the table at Ben-Merari and his entourage. He also saw that Manlius had come up behind him with some documents in his hand. Nicholaus then said, "The contract was entered into by both parties and signed in front of witnesses. They both agreed to the quantity of oil to be sold and the price that was to be paid. There will be no changes made in the arrangement. What has been negotiated, written, and sealed has been negotiated, written, and sealed. That is the end of all negotiations. That is my final decision, and you are welcome to leave. Don't trip over the Roman behind you. He may object."

Ben-Merari was taken aback by the bold abruptness of Nicholaus, and not wishing to become involved with a Roman, he departed along with his entourage in haste.

It's a Girl

Passover had come and gone, with no reports of the Nazarene being in Jerusalem. Temple activity had returned to normal, but their income was down. The priests were still rejoicing and counting their blessings that there were no further challenges from Jesus or his followers. The quiet after a holiday had settled in. Figs were out on the trees in Jerusalem, and Eglah's time has come.

In the northeast residential area of Jerusalem, women do not have babies, the commons* do. The midwives were there and along with Zibiah, Eglah's best friend, and all the women of the Commons had gathered round Eglah, along with Baara, Cozbi, and some of the third-floor ladies. They brought with them booties, caps, blankets, and swaddling clothes. Someone had even brought a cradle. All that and more had been prepared for this marvelous day of birthing.

The men of the commons had gathered on the grounds in support of Levi. Tables had been set up. Food and wine were prepared, and merriment was being shared by all, in expectation of that marvelous moment of birth. All the men hoped for a boy, but girls do happen.

After what seemed to be an eternity, a baby's cry could be heard coming from Levi's house, and Zibiah reported joyfully, "It's a girl!" The men of the commons rejoiced with Levi with singing and dancing, and then Levi headed into the house to see his new daughter.

The news soon spread to Beth Eden, and all the day's business ceased as the celebration and merriment began. Even the Romans gathered in the first-floor business room along with the ladies of the third floor and joined in the celebration that lasted into the wee hours of the next morning.

Nicodemus doesn't even think about his weekly trip to Beth Eden anymore; he just makes it. Everything looked normal when he entered and made his way to Nicholaus's table.

Lady got up from her camel's blanket and went over for her weekly pat on the head; she licked his hand.

Nicholaus welcomed his friend, and they set down for their morning meal together.

Nicodemus asked if Eglah has had her baby yet.

"Yes. She had it late last week. The whole neighborhood turned up for the event, and even some of the ladies from the third floor where there. It was a girl, and they named her Huldah."

"Huldah, that's quite a name to live up to. Eileithyia* was smiling on them."

"Yes, it is a good name, but she comes from good stock. She can handle it."

"Those two have been in love ever since I first saw them together."

"That wasn't being in love, my friend. That was being in heat. You must understand, being in heat comes first. Then comes the chemistry, and if the heat and chemistry are right, they beget love."

"Love is a living thing. It needs to be nurtured, swaddled,* and fed regularly. It grows, and in time, it suffers through adolescence, and later it still passes into a graceful state of old age. Eventually, they will put that sex thing behind them. Then they will realize what real love is."

"Now that bone is going to take some chewing."

"By the way, I have a new scroll for you. I think you will find this one most interesting." Nicholaus handed the scroll to Nicodemus.

Nicodemus unrolled the scroll and began to read.

Galilean IX

Greetings and may the High Holy One of Israel, blessed is he, bless and keep you. Amen. I, Chelub Bar-Abihail of the tribe of Levi, have sent you three previous scrolls, and now I have witnessed another event here in Capernaum, worthy of a report. This event was first reported to the elders in Sepphoris, and upon their request, I am now forwarding this scroll to you.

A certain slave of a centurion, one dear to him, was very ill and was about to expire. And hearing about Jesus, he sent elders of the Jews to him, asking him that he might come to restore his slave.

The elders came to Jesus and earnestly begged him, saying, "He to whom you give this is worthy, for he loves our nation, and he built a synagogue for us." And Jesus went with them.

But he being yet not far away from the house, the centurion sent friends to him, saying to him, "Lord, do not trouble, for I am not worthy that you come under my roof. For this reason I did not count myself worthy to come to You. But say a word and let my servant be cured. For I also am a man having been set under authority, having soldiers under myself. And I say to this one, 'Go!' And he goes. And to another, 'Come!' And he comes. And to my slave, 'Do this!' And he does it."

And hearing these things, Jesus marveled at him, and turning to the crowd following him, he said, "I say to you, I do not find such faith in Israel."

And those sent, having returned to the house, found the sick slave well. [Luke 7:2–10 from the Greek]

I have nothing more to report at this time.

The Lord bless you and keep you. The Lord make His face to shine upon you and be gracious to you. The Lord lift up his countenance upon you and give you peace. [Num. 6:24–26 from the Hebrew]

Nicodemus looked up with an astonished look on his face: "He healed the servant of the Roman centurion?"

Nicholaus smiled and said, "Yes, it looks like the Baptist did mean Gentiles when he said that redemption was available to the soldiers."

Nicodemus then said he had spoken to the council about Ben-Merari, and they assured him that the situation would be dealt with. With that, Nicodemus excused himself and headed for the council chambers.

*****

Later that afternoon, Bar-Shual came to Beth Eden looking for Nicholaus.

Nicholaus stood up and said, "I am Nicholaus."

Lady stood up, the hair on her back standing up and her tail between her legs. She emitted a low growl. Nicholaus patted her head and said, "It's okay, Lady. It's okay." She still stood at the ready, just in case.

Bar-Shual then said, "I have come from Ben-Caiaphas to pay you the money that is due you, along with a recompense for your trouble."

Nicholaus received the pouch. "Thank you, my friend. And may I ask you your name?"

Sheepishly, he replied, "My name is Bar-Shual, and you have my humble apology for not recognizing your contract." He then humbly excused himself and ran from the building.

21

The Question

A black silk robe studded with diamonds and an occasional ruby gently caressed the cold night sky and had the domain over it. Slowly the black gave way to a thin line of indigo. Clouds revealed their etchings in gray and black. Indigo was pushed up and outward by violet and then red. The bottoms of the clouds were touched with pink as black and then blue gave way to them. Orange appeared dark at first, then lighter as the whole sky exploded with color. The sun peeked over the top of the mountain then promenaded to its majestic throne. The High Holy One of Israel had again fulfilled his promise of a bright new day. "Let the heavens be glad, and let the earth rejoice: and let them say among the nations 'Jehovah reigns'" (1 Chron. 16:31 from the Hebrew).

Baruch Bar-Azariah found enjoyment in watching the sunrise over the water of the Sea of Galilee when he went up to the hill behind his house to recite his first morning prayer. "I give thanks before you, living and eternal King, that you have returned within me my soul with compassion. How abundant is Your faithfulness! The beauty of your creation is beyond the imagination of man. I am not worthy to behold such majesty."

Baruch saw the fisherman putting out for an early morning catch. He prayed for them and their success. The air was filled with the sounds of a stirring family and the odors of fresh-baked bread.

98

Baruch returned to the house and went to the courtyard for his morning meal with his sons.

After the meal, Baruch retired to his study, along with his three sons, for their morning studies and prayer.

Before Baruch could start his lesson, Reaiah, his youngest son, had a question for him. The youngster was always full of questions. "Why does God talk to himself?"

"Your question is out of context with the answer you are seeking." Baruch thought for a while and then got up from the table and went to the cupboard to retrieve two mugs. One was baked earthen from the house of the potter, and the other was brass. Taking a wineskin, he explained, "To find the answer to your question, you must understand creation from the Torah. Each of us are many different people. To you, I am father. To your mother, I am husband. To the fisherman, I am a buyer, and on it goes. Each of us is something to everyone, but never the same to all."

The boys were now paying close attention. Their father did not always respond to questions about "Torah things," so they wanted to hear all he had to say.

"Consider the crack running down the table between you and me as 'in the beginning.'" Baruch said as he started his explanation. "The Torah tells us that in the beginning, God created the heavens and the earth. We are the only ones here, so I am going to call Jehovah 'God' so you understand who it is I am speaking of. My right side, your left, of the crack is before 'in the beginning.' My left side is creation after 'in the beginning.' Before in the beginning, God already was. Creation was his idea from before 'in the beginning.' He knew that creation would consist of two worlds, one spiritual and one earthly. In order to exist in both of these new worlds, God had to separate himself out into two other beings."

Baruch took the wineskin and poured wine into the brass mug. He placed the mug across the table on his right side. "This mug represents God separating out a part of himself as a spiritual being in both the spirit and earthly worlds." He then poured wine into the earthen mug. "This mug represents God separating out a part of himself as an earthly being in both the spirit and earthly worlds." He placed the brass and earthen mug next to each other. "Both mugs are given the attributes of God necessary for fulfilling the duties of their office. Neither of the mugs are given all the attributes of God. These he reserved for himself. So in the beginning, God created the heavens and the earth, and as a result of the precreation plan, God existed in three forms. As you read the Torah, you must place God in his proper context. Which of the three forms of one God is this Scriptures referring to? By keeping the writings in their proper context, you will no longer be confused."

Naam, his second son, then asked, "How do we know which is which? What are their names?"

Baruch replied, "He who is in the earthen mug is God the King that breathed life into Adam and walked with him in the garden. He is also the Captain of the heavenly host that appeared to Joshua. He who is in the brass mug is God the Spirit."

Naam then asked, "What about the prophet from Nazareth? Is he a real prophet? Is he the Messiah?"

Baruch said that he really didn't know. "But time will tell. We just have to wait and watch and listen to find the answer."

Dodai said, "I met him at Uncle Samuel's house up in Capernaum. His name is Jesus."

"Tell us about it," his father said.

"Uncle Samuel invited him and his followers to a feast so he could size him up. Since I was a guest in the house and a member of the family, I was invited to take part in the feast. I had to recline at the other end of the table, so I never had a chance to talk to him or his followers."

Baruch then said that he wanted Dodai to remain in the study after the lessons were over and to write down everything he could remember about what happened and what was said during the feast.

Baruch then continued with the morning class. When the class was over, everyone went their own way, except Dodai, who stayed behind and began to write a scroll.

22

The Widow's Son

Levi, Eglah, Baara, and Cozbi were making their morning rounds in the market along with Zibiah. The third-floor ladies were taking care of the baby and enjoying every minute of it. Levi spotted Ben-Merari and pointed him out to Eglah. Levi said that he was the one that had been stirring up trouble for her and the girls with the merchants. As they were looking at him, they saw him kick a blind beggar. Then they saw Manlius come up behind him and give him a big kick in his behind that lifted him right up off the ground. Eglah gasped at the sight and the girls giggled. Ben-Merari got his balance and turned around to confront his attacker, only to find that he was looking at the blade of a Roman short sword right in front of his nose. "If I ever see you kick someone like that again, it won't be my foot. It will be this gladius going up your behind," the Roman threatened as he waved his sword in Ben-Merari's face.

Ben-Merari, bowing and apologizing, backed away. He and his entourage hurriedly left the market.

Levi smiled and Egla. The girls laughed out loud at seeing what had happened to Ben-Merari. *It's a joy to see someone get what's coming to them*, Eglah thought.

After they had completed their shopping, they returned to the commons, and the girls went on to Beth Eden.

Together, Levi and Eglah, and with Zibiah's help, dug a small hole behind their house and planted a pine tree that they had purchased at the market. This was the custom. When a boy was born, a cedar tree was planted, and when a girl was born, a pine tree. When they grew up and married, the wedding canopy was made of branches taken from both the girl's and the boy's trees.

*****

Nicholaus received a new scroll writer. He introduced himself as Joseph Bar-Lecah of Nain. The middle-aged man was dressed like a man of means. He spoke Greek like a businessman, with very little Galilean accent.

Lady got up and walked over to him to give him her greetings.

Bar-Lecah patted Lady on the head and said, "It doesn't make any difference how much or how little you have. Having a good dog makes you rich."

Lady returned to her blanket behind Nicholaus's chair to lie back down.

Nicholaus thanked Bar-Lecah for his comment and offered him food and drink, and then he asked him about the latest news from Nain and the Valley of Jezreel.

Bar-Lecah executed the normal rituals and helped himself to that which was offered. He said, "It has been a good year for crops, and the flocks are large and fat. There's already snow on top of Mount Tabor so their water supply is assured for next year. There is a movement in Nain to increase taxes to allow for the housing and feeding of the poor. I have not made up my mind on this issue. I wonder what you have to say about it."

Nicholaus considered the question and then replied, "I saw this tried once down in Kadesh Barnea. It didn't work."

"We cannot right social ills by taking from one what he has honestly acquired in order to give it to another that has not earned it. This is as slippery as the slopes of Mount Tabor in the mid of winter, and once it's in place, two things are going to happen. The first is that people collecting the taxes and distributing to the poor are going to get rich off your tax money. The second is once the poor start getting something for nothing, they're going to keep wanting more and more and more. My rule is treating others the way you would like to be treated. Treat yourself the way you would treat others. And don't do for others what they can do for themselves."

"Don't do for others what they can do for themselves. Are you suggesting it would be better to develop a works program that will give the poor a job so they can make their own way?"

"No. But now that I think about it, that might be a good idea."

Bar-Lecah thanked Nicholaus for his commentary and said that he was going to take them to the elders in Nain.

*****

The next day, Nicodemus felt a chill in the late-morning breeze as he hurried along to Beth Eden. Upon entering, he was happy to see there was no one at Nicholaus's table. He seated himself and reached for a mug of wine.

"Good news, my friend. I have a scroll for you down from Galilee. It came from Nain." With that he handed Nicodemus the scroll.

Galilean X

Greetings in the name of Jehovah, the High Holy One of Israel. I am Joseph Bar-Lecah, a Pharisee of the tribe of Judah. I have contacted the elders in Sepphoris about the following. I am now sending you this report, on their advice.

There was a funeral here in the city of Nain, and I was one of the pallbearers. We were carrying out the only son of a widow, who had died. And a considerable crowd of the city was with her. A man, we later identified as Jesus of Nazareth, said to her, "Stop weeping." And coming up, he touched the coffin, and we all stood still. He said, "Young man, I say to you, arise!" And the dead

one sat up and began to speak. And he gave him
to his mother. Fear took hold of all, and we glorified God saying, "A great prophet has risen up
among us and God has visited his people" [Luke
7:12–16 from the Greek].

The Lord bless you and keep you. The Lord
make His face to shine upon you and be gracious
to you. The Lord lift up his countenance upon
you and give you peace [Num. 6:24–26 from the
Hebrew].

Nicodemus rolled up the scroll and placed it in his robe.

Looking at Nicholaus, Nicodemus said, "He didn't even know
her, and no one asked him to intervene."

Nicholaus replied, "Yes, but now the question is, did he do it
out of compassion or to enhance and spread his reputation?"

Nicodemus left and headed for the secretary's office, where he
gives the scroll to Abner Ben-Hilkiah, the council secretary.

After reading the contents of the scroll, the secretary said: "Nain.
This is the first time we have had a report from there. I guess there is
no question that the boy was dead. Bar-Lecah was a pallbearer. But
there is still no information about the Nazarene's background. Who
is he? Is he of the house of David? We are just not getting the information we need."

*****

That afternoon, Eglah came in to see Levi. She had the baby
lashed to her breast with a woolen sash. Everyone on the floor gathered around to see the baby. Even Manlius and some of his friends
came out from the Roman room. Lady came over to give her greetings, and Eglah knelt down so Lady could see the baby. Lady sniffed
the baby and then gave her a doggy kiss on the cheek, and the baby
giggled with delight.

After things settled down, Nicholaus had both Levi and Eglah
sit down at his table. "This situation with Jesus of Nazareth has devel-

oped to the point that we have to have someone in Nazareth to get us more information. To that end, I want to send Levi to Nazareth, but I won't do it without your approval, Eglah.

Eglah pondered the question and then replied, "I want to know more about this Jesus myself. Mistress Abishag and the ladies and the girls can help me with the baby, and Daniel can escort me to the market, if that is all right with you?"

Nicholaus and Levi indicated that it was.

"In that case, I will be all right while he is gone. Yes, I agree, we need more information, and Levi is just the person to get it."

"Okay, then it is settled, that is, if you're willing to go?"

Levi said that he was eager to go. He wanted to find the answers just as much as anyone else did.

With that, Eglah took the baby up to the third floor for the ladies to see, with Lady running along behind. Levi started preparing for his trip.

Meanwhile, Simon Ben-Cleopas, the indentured servant of Simon Bar-Gaal, came in and headed for Nicholaus's table. He was greeted as an old friend and invited to take seat. "I have a scroll from Bar-Gaal, and this will be the last one I bring down."

"Why? What happened? Did someone demand that Bar-Gaal stop sending scrolls to Jerusalem?"

"No, no, nothing like that. Besides, there is no man alive that could stop my master from steering up trouble whenever he can. This is my last week of indentured service to Bar-Gaal, and I am happy to be heading home to Emmaus so I can take a warm bath for my old tired bones. But tell me, what is your evaluation of this Jesus of Nazareth?"

"We are still investigating the situation and opinions. There are some who are convinced that he is the Messiah, the anointed one of God. There are others that think he is a prophet, and some like Bar-Gaal, think he is just another charlatan. But most have not made up their minds yet. So tell me, what are you going to do when you get home?"

"My father has a shop in Emmaus, and I will be working with him."

Small talk followed along with a time of refreshment. When Simon Ben-Cleopas was ready to leave, Nicholaus wished him good luck on his new adventure and God's speed on his journey.

Anointed by a Sinner

Nicodemus was always happy to spend his once-a-week morning with his friends. He entered Beth Eden with a smile on his face, a warm greeting for his friend Nicholaus, and a pat on the head for his friend Lady.

Nicholaus got up from his chair and shared in the greetings.

Lady curled up on her blanket as the men seated themselves and enjoyed their morning meal together. Eventually a new scroll was taken from the stack on the table and given to Nicodemus.

Nicodemus then unrolled the scroll and began to read.

Galilean XI

I Simon Bar-Gaal, the Pharisees of Pharisees and Teacher of teachers, here in Capernaum, wish to submit another report on false prophet Jesus of Nazareth.

In order to test him, I invited the false prophet to a dinner in my home. Within the gathering, witnessing the feast was a woman, who was a sinner in the city. Taking an alabaster* vial of ointment and standing behind him, she began to wash his feet with tears. She was wiping with the hair of her head. She ardently kissed his feet and was anointing them with the ointment. If he were a prophet, he would know who and what the woman who touched him was, for she is a sinner. [Luke 7:36–39 from the Greek]

I am satisfied that this Jesus of Nazareth is a false prophet, and again I am imploring you to do something about him.

Nicodemus rolled up the scroll and placed it in his robe "Anointed by a sinner, and he allowed her to continue until she was finished. Some will say that Bar-Gaal is right in his assessment. On the other hand, does not this show that the people love him?"

"Yes, it does, but somehow I can't help but feel that this report is incomplete. I would like to have heard the rest of the conversation."

*****

Nicodemus hurried down the valley road on his way to the council chambers. He saw an old friend of his coming from the other direction, and he stopped and gave him a Pharisee's greetings. "Baruch, my old friend, how is everything up in Galilee?"

"Fine, fine, my old friend. There are more fish this year than ever. My wife is fine, and the boys are growing like stocks of corn."

The small talk continued for a minute or two, and then each conclude their greetings and go their separate ways.

Nicodemus entered the council's building and headed straight for the secretary's office. Shimon Ben-Gamaliel was there as was Joseph, his old friend from Arimathea.

Ben-Gorion handed the scroll to Ben-Gamaliel, who unrolled it and began to read it out loud. When he had finished, the secretary was the first to speak.

"There is no proper greeting, and I wonder if Bar-Gaal was prompted by the council to have this dinner, or did he do it on his own?"

"Ben-Adon said that he thought the report was incomplete, and he would like to have heard the rest of the conversation."

Ben Gamaliel then offered, "Knowing Bar-Gaal, I am surprised that she even got in the house."

Joseph kept his peace but pondered the report in his heart.

*****

Baruch Bar-Azariah entered Beth Eden and went directly to the table of Nicholaus.

Nicholaus arose with warm greetings. Lady jumped up from her place and, wagging all over, gives her greetings to Baruch.

The men sat down as Baruch gives Lady a good belly rub. "There's nothing like a good dog to make your day."

The men helped themselves to some bread, fruit, and wine.

Baruch committed, "As long as you have figs on your table, everyone will want to be your friend."

The two men laughed and then got down to business.

Baruch produced two scrolls from his robes. He handed one of them to Nicholaus and said, "This is a list of contracts I will be needing as soon as you can write them for me. I think all the information you need is listed with each request."

Handing him the second scroll, Baruch said, "This scroll is from my son Dodai. I sent him up to Galilee on a buying trip, and he was staying in the home of my brother-in-law, Simon Bar-Gaal. While he was there, he met a prophet from Nazareth that Simon had invited to a feast. I instructed Dodai to write down everything he remembers about the feast and what the Prophet and Simon did and had to say to each other. This scroll is what he wrote. I know about the inquiry you sent up to us concerning the Baptist and the sandal man. I don't know if this is the information you want or not, but I thought it worthy of your evaluation."

Nicholaus took the scroll and observed that it was written in Aramaic, so he set it aside to be worked on later.

Baruch thanked Nicholaus for his hospitality and excused himself as he turned to leave.

*****

The next morning, Joseph Ben-Caiaphas was in his study, enjoying his morning time of meditation and prayer. His solitude was interrupted by Jabin Ben-Geber, his first secretary. "What is the situation that brings you to me at this time of day?"

"Please excuse me, Master, but I was given a situation that requires an authority higher than my own to resolve. The scribe Judah Ben-Paruah entered into a contract to loan 10,000 denarii to the Pharisee Tobiel Ben-Shobai. The contract was written by the mediator Joseph Ben-Uzziah, who died shortly after the agreement was entered into. There are two copies of the agreement. One is in Greek, and the other is in an obscure dialect called Syriac. The Greek copy appears to be a standard loan contract, and I can find no one who can read the Syriac copy. The contract calls for a repayment of 12,000 denarii at 100 denarii per month. The widow claims that repayment of the loan was supposed to have been forfeited, with no more payments upon the death of her husband. Her husband has been dead some five years now, and she has been paying 100 denarii a month in repayment. The lender is now evicting her from her home in lieu of the payments she can't or won't make. Because this contract is between a ranking scribe and a Pharisee of high rank, the situation has been referred to us to be resolved."

Ben-Caiaphas then said that he knew each of the people involved and the political movements they were part of. He did not want to get involved with making a judgment. "It doesn't make any difference which way this one goes. Political enemies are going to be made." He paused to think about how he could get out of this. "Convene the Council of Fourteen and give the problem to them."

24

The Rest of the Story

Nicodemus was earlier than normal, and he had a hurried step as he made his way to Beth Eden. After he had seated himself, Nicholaus said to him, "Remember when I sent Levi up to Nazareth to investigate Jesus? Well, he has quite a story to tell." Turning to Levi, he said, "Tell Nicodemus what you told me."

Levi pulled his chair over to their table. Then he gave his report. "When I got to Nazareth, I inquired about the family of the prophet Jesus. The first thing I was told is that Jesus is no prophet but that I should seek out James the carpenter, who is his brother. I located the carpenter shop of James and found that both he and his mother Mary had nothing to say to me. After more inquiry, I found that James has some other brothers.

"One of his brothers, Simon, would talk to me, and he told me that his father Joseph was of the house of David. It seems there was an enrollment made when Quirinius was governor of Syria some thirty or so years ago, and his father insisted that he and his mother had to go to Bethlehem for this enrollment, even though they could have enrolled in Nazareth, because he was of the house of David.

"He also told me that when his mother was with child, she went to visit her cousin Elizabeth who was also with child. Elizabeth, who is from the house of Aaron, is the wife of Zacharias the priest. She stayed with them until Elizabeth gave birth to her son whom they named John. Now when Zachariah was serving in the temple at the altar of incense, he was struck dumb. When the baby was born, the people thought he should be named Zachariah after his father.

"Elizabeth insisted that his name is John. They signed to Zachariah as to what that baby's name should be. And Zachariah spoke for the first time since he came out from the altar of incense. He said that his name is John. This indicates to me that Jesus is of the house of David, and he is also of the house of Aaron, which makes him eligible to be both a priest in the line of Aaron and a king of Israel in the line of David. I am satisfied that Jesus of Nazareth meets all the requirements set down by the scriptures to be the Messiah."

Nicodemus was stunned by this report. At first, he doesn't know what to say. After a moment, he recovered and told them that the council was looking for information like this from Nazareth. He requested that Levi write it up as a scroll and submit it to the council.

After much discussion between the three, Nicholaus then handed Nicodemus a scroll and suggested that the council may want to look into the situation in Capernaum.

Nicodemus looked at Nicholaus with a puzzled look on his face. He then opened the scroll and began to read.

Galilean XII

To the governing council of elders in Jerusalem. Greetings from Galilee in the name of the High Holy One of Israel. May His blessings be upon you.

I, Dodai Bar-Azariah, send you this report at the request of my father, Baruch Bar-Azariah, a member of the Ruling Council of Elders in Sepphoris.

I was present in the home of my uncle Simon Bar-Gaal when he entertained a prophet from Nazareth with a feast. The following is what I saw and heard of the conversation between the prophet and Uncle Simon as I remember it.

All of us were reclining at the table, enjoying our food. The prophet was at the head of the table with his followers on his right. My uncle was on his left side with all his other special guests. I was reclining at the other end of the table. All the town's people had come out to see and hear the event.

There was a woman standing behind the prophet weeping, and she knelt down at his feet. I could not see what she was doing, but in a while, I could smell the aroma of a sweet-smelling ointment.

The prophet, speaking to my uncle, said, "Simon, I have something to say to you."

My uncle said, "Teacher, say it."

Then the Prophet said, "There were two debtors to a certain creditor. One owed 500 denarii, and the other 50. But they did not have a thing to pay. He freely forgave both of them. Then which one do you say will love him more?"

My uncle Simon replied, "I suppose the one he forgave the most."

The prophet then said to him, "You have judged rightly." Then turning to the woman, he said to my uncle, "Do you see this woman? I came into your house. You did not give me water for my feet, but she washed my feet with her tears and wiped them off with the hairs of her head. You gave me no kiss. But she, from when I entered, has not stopped fervently kissing my feet. You did not anoint my head with oil, but she anointed my feet with ointment. For this reason I say to you, her many sins are forgiven, for she loved much. But to whom little is forgiven, he loves little."

And he said to her, "Your sins are forgiven. Your faith has saved you. Go in peace." [Luke 7:40–50 from the Greek]

This is all I remember seeing and hearing.

The Lord bless you and keep you. The Lord make His face to shine upon you and be gracious to you. The Lord lift up his countenance upon you and give you peace. [Num. 6:24–26 from the Hebrew]

Nicodemus dropped his arms, the scroll lying in his lap. With a look of astonishment on his face, he exclaimed, "He lied to us. Simon Bar-Gaal lied to us!"

"No, he didn't lie. He just didn't tell all the truth. He allowed his preconceived opinions and arrogance of station to cloud his judgment. I think in the future, we are going to have to be careful in our evaluations of anything he sends us," Nicholaus replied.

Nicodemus rolled up the scroll and paid Nicholaus his dues. In bewilderment, he left Beth Eden and headed for the council chambers.

*****

The Council of Fourteen met later that day in their chambers at the home of Caiaphas.

Jabin Ben-Geber, the first secretary, laid out the problem for the council.

"The scribe Judah Ben-Paruah entered into a contract to loan 10,000 denarii to the Pharisee Tobiel Ben-Shobai. The contract was written by the mediator Joseph Ben-Uzziah, who died shortly after the agreement was entered into. There are two copies of the agreement. One is in Greek, and the other in what is believed to be Syriac. The Greek copy appears to be a standard loan contract. We can find no one who can read the Syriac copy. The contract calls for a repayment of 12,000 denarii. The widow claims that repayment of the loan was supposed to have been forfeited, with no more payments due, upon the death of her husband.

The Syriac copy was then passed around to all of the Fourteen, and none of them could read it. The council debated the question and decided that they did not want anything to do with it. A suggestion was offered that a special investigative court be convened to hear the complaints and report their findings.

According to the Written Law governing the Sanhedrin, the court was to be made up of three people since it involved a loan. The council then decided that one of the judges was to be a scribe, one was to be a Pharisee, and one was to be a mediator. This way all three groups would be represented by one of their peers. The question now became who should be appointed to the court. The name of Jonathon Ben-Jadon, a member of the Sanhedrin, was put forth as the scribe. The Secretary of the ruling Council of Pharisees Abner Ben-Hilkiah was put forward as representing the Pharisees. After the offering of several names and some lengthy debate, the name of Awnee Ben-Adon was accepted to represent the mediators.

It was decided that the court should convene in the chambers of the Council of Fourteen at their earliest convenience. They were empowered by the council, with the approval of the chief priest and the Sanhedrin, to examine evidence, call witnesses, and do whatever else they deemed necessary to come to a conclusion concerning the contract.

With that, the council sent runners out to the three court appointees to ask them if they would be willing to serve and to render onto them all the information that was presently available to the council. The runners were required to report back to the council secretary as soon as possible with the appointees' answers. With that, the council adjourned, and the members were happy that they could pass this situation to someone else, the same way as it had been passed on to them.

Beelzebub

Levi and Eglah were happy to stop by the shop of Towb Ben-Rawkal, an old friend of Nicholaus. He had a glorious greeting for them and invited them to the back of his shop for some refreshment. After a time of relaxation, they went back into the shop, and Levi bought a new robe and shawl for Eglah. They excused themselves and went on with their shopping.

*****

Nicholaus was concerned about his appointment to the special investigative court as authorized by the Council of Fourteen. Both the chief priest and the Sanhedrin had given their approval for the appointments and the arrangements. He was considering the ramifications of this appointment when Nicodemus came in and seated himself at his table. Nicholaus desired to keep his apprehensions to himself. He greeted his friend, and they shared their weekly morning meal together. After a time of relaxation, Nicholaus stated that he had a scroll.

Nicodemus took the scroll, unrolled it, and began to read.

Galilean XIII
Greetings in the name of the High Holy One of Israel.

I am Beri Bar-Beracah, a Pharisee of the tribe of Asher. I dwell in the town of Arbela, and I witnessed the following when I was in Capernaum.

I was in the crowd, observing Jesus of Nazareth. Then one demon-possessed was brought to him, blind and dumb, and He healed him, so that the blind and the dumb could both speak and see.

"Is this not the son of David?" the people around me asked.

Upon hearing, the Pharisees from Jerusalem said, "This one does not cast out demons, except by Beelzebub, ruler of the demons."

Jesus then said to them, "Every kingdom divided against itself is brought to ruin. And every city or house divided against itself will not stand. And if Satan throws out Satan, he is divided against himself. How then will his kingdom stand? And if I throw out the demons by Beelzebub, by whom do your sons throw them out? Because of this, they shall be your judges. But if I cast out the demons by the Spirit of God, then the kingdom of God has come to you. Or how is it anyone able to enter into the house of a strong one and plunder his goods unless he first tie up the strong one and then he will plunder his house?

"He who is not with me is against me, and he who does not gather with me scatters. Because of this, I say to you: Every sin and blasphemy shall be forgiven to men, but the blasphemy concerning the Spirit shall not be forgiven to men. And whosoever speaks a word against the Son of man, it shall be forgiven him. But whoever speaks against the Holy Spirit, it shall not be forgiven him, not in this age, nor in the coming one." [Matt. 12:22–32 from the Greek]

He had more to say, but I can't remember what it was.

Nicodemus lowers the scroll to his lap. "That man continues to amaze me. Is there anything he can't do? A house divided against itself will not stand? How can one divide our house except through rebellion? Does the son ever set in judgment of his father, except in rebellion? And speaking against the Holy Spirit? These Pharisees may live to regret their charge of Satan throwing out Satan."

"I think He is saying that the process of casting out demons involves a process invoking the power of the Holy Spirit, and speaking against it would amount to blasphemy. He is also indicating that Satan has a spiritual kingdom of his own that is in direct conflict with the spiritual kingdom of God. Also there is an indication that there is no neutral. If one is not in one kingdom, he is in the other."

Nicodemus then took up the scroll, found his place, and continued to read.

Some of the scribes and Pharisees answered him, "Master, we would see a sign from thee."

But he answered and said unto them, "An and evil and adulterous generation seeks after a sign, and there shall no sign be given to it but the sign of Jonah the prophet: for as Jonah was three days and three nights in the belly of the whale so shall the Son of Man be three days and three nights in the heart of the earth [Matt. 12:38–39 from the Greek]

The Lord bless you and keep you. The Lord make His face to shine upon you and be gracious to you. The Lord lift up his countenance upon you and give you peace. [Num. 6:24–26 from the Hebrew]

"Three days and three nights in the heart of the earth? What is that supposed to mean? Is he going to die and be resurrected? How are we supposed to know the sign has been fulfilled? I just don't understand this man."

Levi then spoke up to the astonishment of both Nicholaus and Nicodemus. "Maybe the fulfillment of the sign is not physical but spiritual. The scroll was written in Greek. The word *heart* was interpreted from the Greek word *kardis*, which also means the 'thoughts or feelings.' The word *earth* was interpreted from the Greek word *ghay*, which means earth or world. So the interpretation could be 'the thoughts or feelings of the world.'"

Nicholaus then responded, "That is a most astute observation, and if you are right, you have lifted the latch on a whole new thought process."

Nicodemus then says, "Either way, this Jesus of Nazareth has placed himself a step or two above all the other prophets. And by the way, Caiaphas has decided that Jesus is to be done away with."

With that, he excused himself and headed for the council chambers.

*****

Two days later, the special investigative court convened in the home of Caiaphas, in the chambers of the Council of Fourteen. Jabin Ben-Geber was also present, acting as a representative of the Council of Fourteen and as the court's recording secretary. By mutual consent, Jonathan Ben-Jadon was appointed primary investigator and chief judge of the court.

Ben-Geber then presented the council with the two documents in question. It was found that both documents had been written on parchment and that the lower right-hand corner of one of the documents had been torn off. The corner piece contained most of the seal of the Pharisee Ben-Shobai. The documents were received and declared to be the Greek, the Greek fragment, and the Syriac."

It was then decided that the first two witnesses should be the scribe Ben-Paruah and the widow, Shobai. It was also decided that each of the judges should be allowed to have one aid, present in the chambers, to assist them and that the secretary be assigned as many temple guards as he deemed necessary to keep and segregate the witnesses and for such other duties dictated by the court. The court then requested that the secretary send runners to the witnesses, requiring them to appear one week from now. With that, the court recessed for one week, with the proviso that any one of the judges could request the reconvene at any time.

Nicholaus returned to Beth Eden and asked Levi to be his assistant in his duties as a judge.

Levi assured him he would be honored to do so, and he was satisfied that Daniel could escort the girls and take care of things in their absence.

Nicholaus then stressed that all information about the court and its activities was to be kept confidential until after the proceedings were concluded.

Levi said that he understood, but he could not keep such news from Eglah.

Nicholaus agreed to that condition but stressed that they could not tell anyone else about it.

26

Jairus's Daughter

Eglah was so proud of Levi. He was serving the special investigative court as an assistant to his master, Ben-Adon. Levi had cautioned her not to talk to anybody about it. At least not until the trial was over. Eglah was just busting at the seams to tell Zilpah.

She wanted Levi to get a new robe, but Levi was satisfied with the robe that he had. It was relatively new, it was presentable, and it was comfortable. He felt he had no need for a new one. Eglah insisted that he needed a new one to keep up appearances. They stopped at the shop of Towb Ben-Rawkal, and he showed them the very best selection that he had. Picking out a new robe was number one on Eglah's list of things to do that day, and she was happy that they stopped by at Ben-Rawkal's. Levi still didn't think it was necessary, but he gave in to her wishes. He always does.

As they meandered through the market, Eglah was taken by an alabaster vial of ointment. It was very expensive, and Levi bartered it down as far as he could. Eglah made a few request for herself, so Levi got it for her. After all, he just got a new robe and he had been doing very well with his contracts for the last few weeks, and he felt that they could afford it this one time.

*****

Nicodemus was in a hurry to get to Beth Eden. He had heard rumors about the appointment of his friend to be a judge on the special investigative court. Nicodemus wanted to hear all about it. And it was the first thing he asked about when he sat down at the table.

Lady came in the door behind him and curled up on her blanket.

Nicholaus was not too anxious to talk about the court or the trial to follow. He was embarrassed at all the attention it was drawing, and he just felt that it wasn't appropriate. He confirmed that he had received an appointment, but he didn't know much as the court had not been convened yet.

The men had their morning meal together, and the conversation touched on just about everything except the trial. After a while, Nicholaus said that there was a new scroll down from Galilee. He reached over and picked up a scroll from his table and handed it to Nicodemus. Nicodemus opened the scroll and began to read.

Galilean XIV

Greetings and blessings in the name of the High Holy One of Israel.

I, Chelub Bar-Abihail of the tribe of Levi, have sent you previous scrolls. I am sending you this scroll over the objections of Simon Bar-Gaal. This event happened in my presence, and I feel it important enough to report it to you despite his objections and the inevitable repercussions.

Jairus, the ruler of the synagogue, came to Jesus and, falling at his feet, begged him to come to his house. His only daughter was about twelve years old, and she was dying.

As Jesus was going, the crowd pressed in on him. There was a woman who was bleeding for twelve years; she had spent her whole living on physicians but could not be cured by anyone. She came up from behind Jesus and touched the border of his garment. Instantly, the flow of her blood stopped.

And Jesus said, "Who touched me?"

And all having denied, Peter and those with him said, "Master, the crowds press and jostle you. And do you say who has touched me?"

But Jesus said, "Somebody touched me for I know the power had gone out from me."

Seeing that she was not hidden, the woman came trembling and kneeled down before him and told him before all the people for what reason she touched him and how she was instantly cured.

He said to her, "Daughter, be comforted. Your faith has healed you. Go in peace."

As He was yet speaking, someone came from the synagogue said to Jairus, "Your daughter has expired. Do not trouble the teacher."

But Jesus answered him, "Do not fear. Only believe, and she will be healed."

Arriving at the house, he did not allow anyone to enter except Peter, James, John, and the father and mother of the child. All were weeping. But he said, "Stop weeping. She has not died but is sleeping." And they scoffed at him, knowing that she was dead. He ordered them outside. Taking hold of the daughter's hand, he called out, "Child, rise up." Her spirit returned, and she rose up immediately. And he ordered that she be given something to eat. Her parents were amazed. But he charged them to tell no one of that which occurred. [Mark 5:22–43 and Luke: 8:40–56 from the Greek]

This last part I heard standing at the door.

This was not reported to the elders in Sepphoris. I am trusting that you will understand my concerns.

The Lord bless you and keep you. The Lord make his face to shine upon you and be gracious to you. The Lord lift up his countenance upon you and give you peace. [Num. 6:24–26 from the Hebrew]

Nicodemus laid the scroll aside and said, "I see what you mean by a small revolt in Capernaum. The woman was healed by just reaching out and touching his garment."

"No," Nicholaus replied. "The woman was healed by her faith, which was exercised by reaching out to touch his garment."

"What about the daughter? Was she really dead?"

"I have every reason to believe so. The widow's son was raised from the dead, so it's not like he hasn't done it before."

"Yes, I see your point."

Nicholaus then asked, "Is there anyone from Capernaum on the council in Sepphoris?"

Nicodemus said that he did not think so. Nicholaus then suggested that maybe they could use a good Levite. Nicodemus pondered the suggestion as he hurried off to the council chambers.

27

The Testimonies Begin

The court reconvened at the appointed place and time. The secretary reported that both of the witnesses were present in an outer chamber. Chief Judge Ben-Jodan ruled that they were ready to proceed and called the court to order. He called Jonathon Ben-Paruah to be brought forth as a witness.

Jonathon Ben-Paruah was brought in by two of the temple guards assigned to assist the secretary. Ben-Paruah stood before the tribunal, and the temple guard remained standing behind the witness's chair.

The secretary stood and began to read from a scroll he had prepared for each of the witnesses. "It is written in the law of Moses that thou shall not bear false witness [Exodus 20:16 from the Hebrew]. It is also written a false witness shall not be clean and a bearer of lies shall perish" [Prov. 19:9 from the Hebrew]. Then to the witness, he said, "Do you understand and agree with what was written?"

Ben-Paruah said that he did. The secretary told him to be seated in the witness chair.

The chief judge then started the interrogation. "Did you enter into a contract with Tobiel Ben-Shobai for the loan of 10,000 denarii?"

Ben-Paruah said that he did.

Holding up the Greek copy of the contract, he then asked, "Is this the agreement that you entered into?"

Ben-Paruah examined the document and replied, "Yes, it is."

The chief judge then asked the other judges if they had any questions for this witness.

Abner Ben-Hilkiah said that he had one. The Chief Judge nodded to him and then he asked: "How did it happen that the corner of the contract was torn off?"

The witness answered, "The parchment had gotten wet, and when it dried, it was brittle and the corner broke off."

There were no more questions, and with that the witness was excused with the understanding that he was subject to be recalled. He was escorted from the chambers.

The chief judge then called for the widow Ben-Shobai.

The Widow Ben-Shobai was brought in. She stood, visibly trembling, before the tribunal, and the secretary stood and began to read the articles from the scroll. Then addressing the witness, he said, "Do you understand and agree with what was written?"

The Widow Ben-Shobai, with a trembling voice, said that she did.

The chief judge then told her to be seated and started the interrogation. "Did your husband, Tobiel Ben-Shobai, enter into a contract with Tobiel Ben-Shobai for the loan of 10,000 denarii?"

Continuing to tremble, she confirmed that he did.

Holding up the Syriac copy of the contract, he then asked, "Is this the agreement that he entered into?"

She examined the document and replied, "Yes, sir, it is. That is his signet."

"Can you read it for us?"

"No, sir, I cannot."

"Then how do you know what it says?"

"I know because that is what my husband told me what it says."

"I see." The chief judge then asked the other judges if they had any questions for this witness. They indicated that they did not. The witness was excused, subject to recall.

Ben-Adon then asked to see both copies of the contract again as the other two judges conferred with each other. After he handled them, he motioned for Levi to come up and handle them. "What does your gut tell you? What do you feel?"

Levi handled the two documents and then handled the fragment and held them up to the light. He then picked up the Greek and the fragment and examined it with a close critical eye. He then whispered to Nicholaus that he thought that all three were of different parchments and that the edge of the Ben-Shobai signet was not as sharp on the Greek as it was on the fragment.

Nicholaus then asked Levi if it was his opinion that the Greek had been tampered with. Levi assured him that he was sure that it had been. Nicholaus waved Levi back to his seat and returned the documents to the secretary.

The chief judge reviewed the testimony and asked if there were any questions. Finding that there were none, he declared a one-week recess, and everyone went their ways.

When Nicholaus and Levi were out of the chambers and well away from everyone else, Nicholaus told Levi that he had two things for him to do. First he was to talk to the Daniel, who is from the Khabur Valley, and see if he can read and write Syriac. The second thing was to see if he could find a way to make a signet from the imprint of a signet.

Levi said that he understood and that he would get started right away.

*****

Later that day, an elderly man dressed as a Pharisee approached Nicholaus and said that he was here at the urging of Chelub Bar-Abihail. He had witnessed an incident in Capernaum involving the alleged prophet Jesus of Nazareth.

Nicholaus invited the man to set down and enjoy some refreshments. He then examined the scroll and saw that it was a report and that it was written in Aramaic. He gave the scroll to Levi and then asked for the latest news from Capernaum and the ongoing situation between his friend Chelub and Bar-Gaal.

He replied that they were still of different opinions and that his friend's favor has been growing in the community while Bar-Gaal's has been falling. "It seems that Ben-Gaal's student count has been falling, and he is no longer making the money that that he used to make."

Nicholaus gave a polite neutral response, and the conversation was then reduced to small talk.

Imprint of a Signet

Eglah and Levi were making their morning rounds in the market with the girls. Zilpah had the baby. Levi spotted a display of daggers. He stopped and asked the merchant to tell him about the daggers and most particularly about the sharpest ones he had with a near straight edge.

The merchant picked out one and said, "This is a Celtiberian, from Alonis, Contestani. It is made of the finest steel. See the patterns of banding mottling that looks like flowing water. That indicates that this blade is tough and resistant to shattering, and look how sharp it is." With that, the merchant plucked a hair from his head and cut it in two with just one pass of the blade.

Levi was impressed and bought the dagger along with a sheath without haggling over the price. He placed it inside his robe, and they continued with their shopping. He heard about the art of bartering from Eglah when they got home.

When Levi arrived at Beth Eden, he went directly to the Roman room to pick up some request for contracts. The centurion Cornelius from Galilee was visiting, and the conversation was centered around Herod the Tetrarch. It seems that he too was now looking for Jesus of Nazareth. Levi picked up the scrolls and politely excused himself and went back to his table. He told Nicholaus about the conversation he had overheard, and Nicholaus told him to write it up for submission to the council.

Levi set the Romans scrolls aside, selected one, and began to break the seal with his new dagger. The seal did not break but fell off and landed upside down on his table. This didn't happen very often. Levi looked at the seal, and there was the answer to his question. Running down to the middle of the back of the seal was the imprint of the edge of the parchment. If the wax from the seal can imprint the edge of the parchment, why couldn't it be used to create a new signet?

Levi was now deep in thought about his problem. He had tried to seal the imprint of his signet as he would seal a document, only to find that the imprint of the signet had been crushed in the process. He now held the ceiling wax near the flame of a lamp, and let the wax drip into the imprint of his signet, but that didn't work; it just melted the seal. After more deep thought, he then went to the kitchen and returned with a large bowl of water and a small vial of olive oil. He made a new imprint of his signet. He dipped the corner of the parchment with the imprint of his signet into the bowl of water; this hardened the wax. He then allowed oil to drip into it and then turned it upside down to allow the excess to drip off. The next step was to allow wax to drip into the hardened oiled seal to make a copy of the signet on his ring. The results were an exact copy of his signet except the edges were not as sharp. Levi then cut a strip of parchment four fingers wide and then cut the piece in two. He used his signet to impress one of the pieces in the lower right-hand corner and use the wax signet to impress the other in the same place. He showed his results to Nicholaus. Nicholaus examined both imprints and was impressed with his results.

Levi then asked Daniel to join with him and Nicholaus. The two seated themselves in front of Nicholaus. Nicholaus went straight to the point. "You told us that you were from the Kahabur Valley, so tell me, can you read and write Syriac?"

"Yes, Master, I can. It was the language of my youth."

"Excellent. I trust that you know about the tribunal that I am serving on?"

Daniel replied that he had heard something about it.

"Good, I would like to call you as a witness when we reconvened the tribunal. We have a document written in Syriac that no one can read, and you would be doing us a great service if you could come and read it for us."

Daniel assured him that he would be happy to.

*****

Nicodemus came in and seated himself as Bar-Ananiel got up to leave. He and Nicholaus then enjoyed their morning meal and leisure time together.

It was time to get down to business, and Nicodemus asked if there were any scrolls for him today. Nicholaus said yes, there was one and handed him a new scroll.

Nicodemus unrolled the scroll and began to read

Galilean XV

Greetings in the name of the High Holy One of Israel.

I, Michael Bar-Carmi, a Pharisee of Pharisees, reside in Capernaum. I have no desire to become involved in the conflict between two of our leading Pharisees, so I am most reluctant to submit this report to you. I first reported this incident to the elders at Sepphoris and was ordered by them to forward it to you despite my reluctance to do so.

Two blind men were following Jesus of Nazareth, crying out, "Have pity on us, son of David."

And Jesus said to them, "Do you believe that I am able to do this?"

And they said to him, "Yes, Lord."

Then he touched their eyes, saying, "According to your faith, let it be to you." And their eyes were opened. [Matt. 9:27–30a from the Greek]

I have nothing more to report at this time.

The Lord bless you and keep you. The Lord make His face to shine upon you and be gracious to you. The Lord lift up his countenance upon you and give you peace. [Num. 6:24–26 from the Hebrew]

Nicodemus rolled up the scroll and put it in his robe. "They heard him and believed him to be the Son of David. 'According to your faith, let it be to you.' Again, faith was the rope that lifted the latch to open the door. Most interesting."

Nicholaus said that he was reminded of a passage in Isaiah and that he had written it down for him. Opening a scroll from his table, Nicholaus began to read.

"Do not fear, your God will come with vengeance with the full dealing of God. He will come and save you. Then the eyes of the blind shall be opened, and the ears of the death open. Then the lame shall leap like a deer, and the tongue of the dumb shall sing. For waters shall break out in the wilderness and streams in the desert. And the mirage shall become a pool, and the thirsty land shall become springs of water, in the home of the jackals, in its lair, and a place for the read in the rush.

"And a highway shall be there and away, and it shall be called the way of holiness. The unclean shall not pass over it. And it is for them the wayfaring one, yet fools shall not go astray. No lion shall be there, and no violent beast shall go up on it. It shall not be found there. But the redeemed the ones shall walk there. And the ransomed of Jehovah shall return and enter Zion, with singing and everlasting joy. On their head, gladness and joy shall reach them; and sorrow and sighing shall flee." [Isa. 35:4b–10 from the Hebrew]

Nicodemus pondered the reading and then remarked, "You are suggesting the coming of Messiah?"

Nicholaus confirmed that he was. With that, Nicodemus hurried off to the council chambers, with scrolls in hand.

*****

That afternoon, Pekah, the eunuch servant of King Herod the Tetrarch of Galilee, came in to see Nicholaus. He had some request for contracts for him. Nicholaus stood and greeted his friend and spent a good amount of time entertaining him.

"Tell me, what is the latest news of your master?"

"There is nothing new in Tiberius. Antipas still thinks himself a king. He is still infatuated with his stepdaughter, Salome, and the family spends their afternoons in the hot water baths."

"What of the prophet Jesus of Nazareth?"

"Antipas thinks that he may be John the Baptist who has come back from the dead. He is trying to have him arrested, but his guards can't find him."

The conversation was then reduced to small talk, and eventually, Pekah excused himself and left.

The Investigation

The special investigative court convened as requested by the chief judge. The chief judge asked if there was any business to be conducted before they called witnesses. Ben-Adon requested that the court examine the three documents again before witnesses were called. The secretary produced the documents and handed them to Ben-Adon. Ben-Adon then took the documents to the window and asked the other two judges to look at them in the light. He pointed out the scratch marks that are produced when parchment is being prepared and how the scratch marks did not line up between the Greek and the Greek fragment. He then asked them to feel and test the texture of the parchment of the two.

After they had done so, he asked them to judge whether or not they were from the same parchment.

Ben-Adon then returned the documents to the secretary and requested that another table along with an oil lamp and a large bowl of water and a small vial of olive oil be made available to the court to be used later.

The chief judge then reported that Rhodocus Ben-Merari had requested to testify, and without objection, he was ready to call him. There were no objections. The chief judge then nodded to the secretary, and Ben-Merari was escorted into the chambers. The secretary read from the scroll prepared for witnesses. Upon completion, he asked Ben-Merari if he understood and agreed with what was read. Ben-Merari took his seat in the witness's chair, and the chief judge asked him what evidence he had to present to the court.

Ben-Merari spoke with a loud voice that he and Judah Ben-Paruah have been friends since their childhood. He knew of no one more honest and forthright than his friend Ben-Paruah. He then stated that he objected to the presence of a Greek as a judge for this investigation. "This man was worthy of nothing more than selling sponges on sticks*. He failed to treat my friend Ben-Resheph with the justice and the respect due to a man in his station, and he had no business serving as a judge."

Therefore, as far as he was concerned, this whole investigation was contrary to the rules of the Sanhedrin, and its results would be null and void. He then stated he had no more evidence to present.

The chief judge paused before he responded and then stated that first of all, his opinion of Ben-Paruah did not constitute evidence. Second of all, the judges seated in the court had been appointed by the Council of Fourteen and approved by the chief priest. Any objections relating to the judges would have to be taken up with them. The chief judge then ruled that all the testimony given by Rhodocus Ben- Merari was out of order and ill relevant to the question at hand, and it was to be struck out from the record. With that, the witness was excused and escorted from the chamber and the building by the temple guard.

The chief judge then asked if there were any other witnesses to be presented. Abner Ben-Hilkiah said that he had none. Ben-Adon said that he had two and asked that the mediator Daniel Bar-Ananiel be called to testify.

The secretary then caused Bar-Ananiel to be escorted into the chambers. The secretary read from the scroll prepared for witnesses. Upon completion, he asked Bar-Ananiel if he understood and agreed with what was read. Bar-Ananiel said that he did and then took his seat in the witness's chair. The chief judge asked Ben-Adon to question his witness.

Ben-Adon then asked Bar-Ananiel if he was able to read and write Syriac. Bar-Ananiel assured him that he could. He then asked how he acquired this talent. He replied that Syriac was the language of his youth, and it was the first one he had learned. Ben-Adon then asked the secretary to produce the Syriac document and to give it to the witness. He then asked the witness to tell them what the document said. It would not be necessary to read the entire document but to give them the essence of what was written.

Bar-Ananiel studied the document and then said that it was a normal loan contract between a man named Judah Ben-Paruah and a man named Tobiel Ben-Shobai. Ben-Paruah had promised to lend Ben-Shobai the sum of 10,000 denarii. He in turn would repay Ben-Paruah the sum of 12,000 denarii at a rate of 100 denarii a month until the entire sum was repaid. There is also a clause at the end of the contract that says that should Ben-Shobai become disabled to the extent that he cannot work or die before the loan was repaid, the remainder of the loan was to be made null and void and that no further payments would be required. Bar-Ananiel asked if the court had any further questions.

The chief judge then asked if Bar-Ananiel had spoken to anyone about being a witness, and if so, who did he talk to and what was said.

Bar-Ananiel said that he had spoken to Judge Ben-Adon. The judge had asked him if he could read and write Syriac. He told him that he could. He then said that the judge wanted to call him as a witness to read a document for the court, and he said he agreed to do so.

"Did Ben-Adon give you any hint as to the document to be read or as to its contents?"

"No."

The chief judge then asked if anyone else had questions for this witness. And there were none. With that, the witness was excused and escorted from the chambers by the temple guards.

Ben-Adon then asked that the table, the oil lamp and the large bowl of water, and the small vial of oil be brought into the chambers. He then asked that his assistant Levi be called as a witness.

Levi came forward and presented himself to the secretary. The secretary read from the scroll prepared for witnesses. Upon completion, he asked Levi if he understood and agreed with what was read. Levi said that he did. The chief judge then told Ben-Adon that he could question his witness.

Ben-Adon then told Levi to set up his demonstration.

Levi took the table that the guard had just brought in and placed it in front of the table of the chief judge. He then placed the lamp and the large bowl of water and the small vial of olive oil on the table along with two sheets of parchment that he removed from his robe. He then invited the other two judges to bring their chairs to the chief judge's table so they could better observe his demonstration.

Levi then cut a four-finger wide strip from each of the two pieces of parchment. He then cut a four-finger square off from one of the pieces. With this square piece, he made the imprint of his signet, which he gave to the chief judge. The remainder of that piece he cut in two and made a second impression in one of them with his signet. He then repeated the experiment he had developed.

He then cut a four-finger square from the uncut strip and asked the secretary to draw a diagonal line through the square from the upper left-hand corner to the lower right-hand corner. This the secretary did as he was asked and returned the marked corner to him. Levi then took the marked corner and made an impression from the hardened wax signet. He showed this to the judges and asked them to compare the two impressions for accuracy and to note that the sharp edges were somewhat rounded on the impression made by the wax signet. After the judges had examined his display and return them to him, he put the two of them together and then, using his dagger, cut them diagonally to match the Greek and the Greek fragment and handed them to the chief judge. With this, he said that his display was over. The chief judge thanked him and then excused him to go back to his duties.

The chief judge now excused Levi and the other two assistants. After they had left the chambers, the three judges and the secretary arranged their tables together and began to deliberate their findings and then had them recorded by the secretary. After much deliberation and bickering back and forth, the judges finally reached a unanimous decision as to their findings. Their findings were then recorded by the secretary and approved by the judges by each of them imprinting his signet on the report.

After the report was finished, the secretary rolled it up and sealed it with his signet. The report along with the testimonies of the witnesses was now ready to be submitted to the Council of Fourteen.

The first secretary hurried off to the study of Caiaphas, the chief priest. He reported that the special investigative court had completed its work, and he now had their findings along with the testimonies of all the witnesses.

Caiaphas said he did not want to know any more about it until his report was given to the Council of Fourteen. With that, he requested that the Council of Fourteen be convened in one week. He said that he would be present and chair that meeting. He also said that as first secretary, he should make the presentation of the findings of the court.

The first secretary then hurried off to make the necessary arrangements for the meeting.

Herod the Tetrarch

Levi and Eglah were making their morning trip to the market; the girls were helping the ladies with their morning chores. Levi could not help but notice that Eglah's emphasis had changed somewhat. She was no longer as interested in things for the ladies as she was for things for the baby. Daniel had come along with them. He said he needed a new robe, and Eglah's maternal instincts went to work to find him the most perfect robe available.

*****

Nicodemus was his usual happy self. When he entered Beth Eden, he headed for the table of Nicholaus. The two men shared their usual greetings and sat down to enjoy their morning meal. After a while, Nicholaus handed Nicodemus a new scroll, and he began to read

Levi II

To the Council of Ruling Elders in Jerusalem, greetings and May the High Holy One of Israel, blessed is he, bless and keep you. Amen.

I, Levi, the assistant of Ben-Adon, received this verbal report from the Roman centurion

Cornelius from Galilee. Upon the urging of my master, the mediator Awnee Ben-Adon, this report is being forwarded to the council for your consideration.

Nicodemus lowered the report to his lap. "Levi wrote this one? Good for him. I'd rather see him get the money than some of the other people who have been sending us scrolls." He found his place and continued to read.

Herod the Tetrarch heard the fame of Jesus. And he said to his servants that this is John the Baptist. He has risen from the dead, and because of this, powerful works are working in him. Herod had seized John, bound him, and put him into prison because of Herodias, the wife of his brother, Philip. He did this for John said to him, "It is not lawful for you to have her." He desired to kill him, but he feared the multitude because they held him as a prophet.

When a birthday feast for Herod was being held, the daughter of Herodias danced in the midst and pleased Herod. So then he promised with an oath to give her whatever she should ask. By the urging of her mother, she told Herod, "Give me here on a platter the head of John the Baptist." And the king was grieved, but because of the oaths and those who had reclined with him, he ordered it to be given. And he sent his men to beheaded John in the prison. And his head was brought on a platter and given to the girl, who brought it to her mother. [Matt. 14:1–11 from the Greek]

The Lord bless you and keep you. The Lord make His face to shine upon you and be gracious to you. The Lord lift up his countenance upon

you and give you peace. [Num. 6:24–26 from the Hebrew]

Nicodemus then responded that he knew John had been beheaded, but he didn't know the details. "It looks like Salome really did get to Herod. We have been hearing stories. This would be a most interesting report for the Council." With that, he excused himself and went on his way.

*****

Later that morning, Ahikar Bar-Jathan from Cana came in and went directly to the table of Nicholaus. He received the usual warm greeting due a Pharisee. Ahikar seated himself and then helped himself to some bread and cheese. Nicholaus poured himself a mug of wine, and the small talk of the two acquaintances began. Ahikar said that he had a scroll from Nathanael Bar-Tholomew, and gave it to Nicholaus.

Nicholaus unrolled the scroll and saw that it was written in Aramaic, and it had to do with the trip to Tyre and Sidon. He set the scroll aside and gave Ahikar his due. He then asked what the news from Cana was.

Ahikar said that he had been made aware of a movement in the crowd to take Jesus and make him a king. But he withdrew from them and went up into the mountains to be alone. [Matt. 14:22–23 from the Greek]

The idle conversation continued about the beginning of spring and the trip down the Jordan Valley. After a short while, Ahikar thanked Nicholaus for his hospitality and departed.

*****

Later that afternoon, a runner came from the first secretary with a message about the upcoming convening of the Council of Fourteen. Nicholaus was given the date and time and was told that both he, Levi, and the mediator Bar-Ananiel were required to attend.

Levi asked Nicholaus what he thought the council was going to do. Nicholaus said that he didn't know. "I am satisfied that you have proved that the Greek parchment is a forgery, but I am not sure we can convince the Council of Fourteen. Even if we do, they would probably find some way to pass the responsibility on to someone else, the same way they had formed the special investigative court. Politics, my friend. Politics can always put you in a strange Bath House."

The Council of Fourteen

The Council of Fourteen convened at the appointed time for its special meeting with the chief priest Ben-Caiaphas sitting as chairman. The meeting was called to order, and the normal agenda was set aside in favor of the report from the first secretary.

The first secretary, Jabin Ben-Geber, stood up at his table and projecting his voice, saying, "The special investigative court has concluded its business and has forwarded its report to us. The findings of the court are recorded in this scroll." He held the scroll up and then handed it to an attendant to deliver to Ben-Caiaphas.

"Three documents were presented to the court, and five witnesses were called. These are the three documents. For identification purposes they are known as the Greek, the Greek fragment, and the Syriac." He passed them on to Ben-Caiaphas.

"These five scrolls are the testimonies of the five witnesses. The first witness was the scribe Judah Ben-Paruah, the second was the widow Ben-Shobai. The third is unnamed because the chief judge ruled his testimony was inadmissible. The fourth was the mediator Daniel Bar-Ananiel, and the fifth was the mediator Levi, the assistant to Judge Ben-Adon. The scrolls were sealed by me at the time the testimony was given and are present here now for your examination upon request." The secretary then seated himself.

Ben-Caiaphas broke the seal on the scroll and read the report to the council: "The special investigative court convened at the appointed time. The court appointed the scribe Jonathan Ben-Jadon as primary investigator and chief judge. The court was then presented with the three documents in question. For identification purposes, they were identified as the Greek, the Greek fragment, and the Syriac. The court then allowed that each of the judges have one aid, present in the chambers, to assist them. He also ruled that the secretary be assigned as many temple guards as he deemed necessary to guard the court, the witnesses, and to maintain order. The court then recessed for one week.

"For a second time, the court reconvened at its appointed time and brought to order by Ben-Jadon. Judah Ben-Paruah was called as the first witness. He testified that he had entered into a contract with the Pharisee Ben-Shobai for a loan of the sum of 10,000 denarii. Subject loan was to be repaid in the amount of 12,000 denarii, 100 denarius per month until the loan was repaid. The witness was then shown the documents, identified as the Greek and the Greek fragment, and asked if this was the contract in question. He replied that it was. He was then asked how the fragment was torn off, and he replied that the parchment gotten wet and brittle and that the corner broke off. The chief judge asked if there were any more questions, and being none, the witness was excused.

"The widow of Pharisee Ben-Shobai was then called as the second witness. She was asked if her husband entered into the above stated loan agreement. She said that he did. The witness was then shown the document identified as the Syriac and asked if that was the contract that her husband agreed to. She said that it was and pointed out his signet on the document. She was asked if she could read the agreement. She said she could not. She was then asked how she knew what it said, and she replied that her husband told her. She was asked what you're her husband told her about the payback. She said that if he was to die before the loan was repaid, all payments were to stop, and the remainder of the loan was to be considered null and void.

Being no more witnesses to be called at this time, Ben-Jadon asked if there was any other business to be conducted. The Judge

Ben-Adon then asked to examine all three documents. This he was allowed to do with that. The chief judge declared a one-week recess. The court convened for a third time, as appointed, to hear from three more witnesses whom had been called. The first unnamed witness gave his testimony, which was ruled inadmissible. "The second witness, the mediator Daniel Bar-Ananiel was called. Judge Ben-Adon questioned the witness and asked if he could read Syriac. The witness said that he could. The secretary then produced the Syriac documents, and the witness told the court that the document in question was a common loan agreement and that Ben-Paruah had promised to lend Ben-Shobai 10,000 denarii. He in turn would repay 12,000 denarii at a rate of 100 denarius a month. The contract also had a clause that said that should Ben-Shobai become disabled, to the extent that he could not work, or if he were to die before the loan was repaid in full, the remainder of the load at the time of his disability or death was to be made null and void with no further payments required. "The chief judge then asked if there were any more questions for this witness, and being none, the witness was excused. Judge Ben-Adon then requested that the mediator Levi be called as the fifth and final witness. The mediator Levi demonstrated to the court how a duplicate signet could be made and how it could be used to forge a document.

"It is the findings of the special investigative court that the loan contract in question was entered into. The witness Judah Ben-Paruah forged a new document and gave a false testimony as to the content of the original. Further, it was found that the witness Judah Ben-Paruah caused the widow of Pharisee Ben-Shobai to pay 100 denarii a month for five years and two months after her husband died. This amount, 6,200 denarii, was collected in violation of the original contract. With this, the court published its findings and forwarded them to the Council of Fourteen. The court then adjourned, to be recalled at the pleasure of the council."

Caiaphas rolled up the scroll and placed it on his table. "You now have a decision to make. You can either resolve the situation or pass it on to the full Sanhedrin. Your choice."

The Council of Fourteen decided that they preferred to deal with it themselves. Based on the testimony and the evidence present, they decided that the witness Judah Ben-Paruah is guilty of forging a sealed document and giving false testimony. He should be required to return the 6,200 denarii overpayment and an additional 12,000 denarii, the amount of the original payback, to the widow of Pharisee Ben-Shobai. Further, he should be stripped of all offices, elected or appointed, that he was currently serving and restricted from ever holding any office, elected or appointed, again. All other punishments prescribed by law were suspended, with the understanding that the Council of Fourteen could inflict the full punishment (death) at any time of their choosing. This decision was unanimous among the Fourteen and was executed under the authority of the chief priest and the Council of Fourteen. The captain of the temple guard was charged with collecting 18,200 denarii from Ben-Paruah and giving it to the widow Shobai.

With this, the council adjourned.

Isaiah Prophesied

Levi and Eglah and the girls came into Beth Eden. Eglah and the girls headed upstairs with the baby and all their packages filled with hidden treasures that they found in the market. Levi came to his table. When Lady saw Levi, she jumped up and ran for the stairs. Nicholaus looked up and said, "Now where is that dog going?" But he was not really expecting an answer.

Levi said that she's going upstairs to be with the baby. "Anytime the baby is around, Lady thinks she has to be her protector. I'm surprised she doesn't come home with us at night."

Nicholaus chuckled and thought, *Maternal instincts at work.*

*****

Nicodemus was happy to see a scroll from Bar-Tholomew. He only wished that there would be more of them so they could understand the inner workings of the Nazarene and his inner circle of followers. Enthusiastically, he began to read.

Nathanael I

May the Blessings of the High Holy One of Israel be with you and yours in your going out and in your coming in.

I, Ahikar Bar-Jathan, from Cana, am the writer of this account. I recorded it as it was given to me by Nathanael Bar-Tholomew, one of the twelve disciples of the Nazarene.

He was with his master when a delegation that was sent from Jerusalem sought him out. Upon finding him, we asked him, "Why do your disciples transgress the traditions of the elders? For they do not wash their hands when they eat bread."

But he said to them, "Why do you also transgress the commandment of God on account of your tradition? For God commanded, 'Honor your father and mother, and he who speaks evil of father or mother by death let him die.' But you say, 'Whoever says to the father or the mother, "A gift (to God), whatever you would gain from me," in no way honors his father or his mother. And you made void the command of God on account of your tradition. Hypocrites! Well, did Isaiah, prophesied by you, say, 'They honor me with their lips, but their heart is far from me, and their fear of me is taught by the command of man.'"

And calling near the crowd, he said to them, "Hear and understand it is not that which enters into the mouth that defiles the man, but that which goes forth out of the mouth, this defiles the man." [Matt. 15:1–11 from the Greek]

The Lord bless you and keep you. The Lord make His face to shine upon you and be gracious to you. The Lord lift up his countenance upon you and give you peace. [Num. 6:24–26 from the Hebrew]

"Hypocrites? He called us hypocrites? How dare he attack us like that? No wonder Caiaphas wants them to do away with him."

Nicholaus jumped to his defense. "What did he say that was a lie? Don't your young followers delight and brag about their 'gifts to God,' and should they not have given those gifts to their father and mother who have no other income? Which comes first, the commandment or the tradition?"

"You may be right, but I'm going to do you a favor, I'm not going to tell the council that you said so. And by the way, the story of your part in the special investigative court was well received by the council and they have reconsidered your suggestion that Chelub Bar-Abihail be appointed to the Council of Ruling Elders in Sepphoris. They are sending a delegation up there to make that appointment. Congratulations, your favor with the council has increased."

*****

Later, Manlius sauntered up to Nicholaus's table, seated himself, and said that he had a question for him.

Nicholaus smiled, poured himself a goblet of wine, and asked him what it was.

"Our astrologers are following up on a report that was recorded some thirty-three years ago. It seems that in the fall of the year 747 (year of Rome), there was a conjunction of the planets Jupiter and Saturn in the constellation of Pisces.* These two planets along with Mars followed each other across the sky until the spring of 748. At that time, they sink below the horizon in the west. Mars was on top of Jupiter on top of Saturn in a straight line pointing straight up and straight down. The astrologers calculated that this won't happen again for about another 1,450 years. They sent the question to Alexandria.

"After combing their records, the astrologers in Alexandria replied that the same event had been recorded there and their calculations for a repeat of the event are just about the same. No one in Alexandria or Rome will speculate on the significance of these events. The question is, would these events have any significance to the Hebrews?

"I know from my studies that Pisces has a great significance to us, but I have no idea what the significance of such a conjunction

149

might be. I'm not into astrology, and quite frankly, I don't believe in it. I'm afraid you're going to have to give your question to someone else."

"Who do you suggest?"

"The religious won't be able to help you. Try the Herodias or someone from Herod's court. They might be able to help."

With that, the Roman went back to his duties.

*See the Astronomy Scroll.

Down from the Mountain

Levi and Eglah and the girls were making their morning meanderings when they became aware of a great commotion in the market. It seems that there was a scuffle, pushing, and shoving between some Pharisees and what seemed to be Zealots.

Five of the Pharisees were stabbed, and when the Romans intervened, one of them was stabbed too. Four of the attackers were placed under arrest, and the rest just disappeared into the crowd. Eglah was relieved that Levi was with her and the girls. She was also glad that the Romans were on the job.

*****

Nicodemus couldn't help but notice that the fall air was getting chilly. He quickened his step as he made his weekly trip to Beth Eden. Upon entering, he was happy to see there was no one with Nicholaus. He went to the table seated himself and helped himself to a goblet of wine.

"Good news, my friend. I have another scroll from Bar-Jathan." Nicholaus handed him the scroll.

Nathanael II

May the Blessings of the High Holy One of Israel be with you and yours in your going out and your coming in.

I, Ahikar Bar-Jathan, from Cana, am the writer of this account as it was given to me by Nathanael Bar-Tholomew.

Jesus, Peter, James, and John went up on a mountain to pray. They were up there overnight. When they came down, a huge crowd had gathered. And behold, a man called aloud from the crowd, saying, "Teacher, I beg you to look at my son because he is my only born. And behold a spirit takes him and he suddenly cries out, and it throws him into convulsions, with foaming. And it departs from him with pain, bruising him, and I begged your disciples that they cast it out, and they were not able."

Jesus answered, "Oh, unbelieving and perverted generation, how long shall I be with you and bear with you? Bring your son here."

But as he was yet coming up, the demon tore him, and he convulsed violently. But Jesus rebuked the unclean spirit and healed the child and gave him back to his father, and all were astounded at the majesty of God. [Luke 9:37–43 from the Greek]

The Lord bless you and keep you. The Lord makes His face to shine upon you and be gracious to you. The Lord lift up his countenance upon you and give you peace. [Num. 6:24–26 from the Hebrew]

Nicodemus then asked, "How could his disciples be with him for this moment in time and not believe they could cast out demons?"

"It was not the disciples, but the father's unbelief in the powers of the Holy Spirit working through the disciples. He was putting his faith in the physical Jesus. Remember what Levi said before that we must learn to read with spiritual eyes and not physical. The father only believed in the physical Nazarene and not in the Holy Spirit working through his followers."

Nicodemus pondered this response as he finished his morning meal. After a short time of small talk, he paid Nicholaus his dues, excused himself, and departed for the council chambers, meeting Lady along the way as she returned from her morning exploration of the streets.

*****

Later that afternoon, Nicholaus delivered some scrolls to Manlius. "Tell me, what was all the excitement in the market this morning?"

"My men had to break up a small riot. It seems that Ben-Merari and his followers were jostling people in the market as usual. Some of the people that they pushed aside were Zealots. One of the Zealot's their leader was named Bar-Abbas and the others that we captured were named Bar-Achan, Bar-Dimas, and Bar-Gestas.

"The Zealots pushed back, and in the ensuing scuffle, both Ben-Merari and Ben Resheph and three others were stabbed by the Zealots. When my men intervened, one of them was stabbed too. Two of the Pharisees, Ben-Merari and Ben Resheph, died of their wounds, but the doctors told me that the other three and my man are going to live. The Zealots Bar-Abbas, Bar-Achan, Bar-Dimeus, and Bar-Gestas were placed under arrest and are now in the dungeon at the Antonia Fortress, awaiting crucifixion. Quite frankly, I will be happy to be rid of all of them. By the way, I have another question for you. What can you tell be about Sukkot?"

"Sukkot, or Tabernacles, has a dual significance historically and agriculturally. Historically, Sukkot commemorates the children of Israel wandering in the desert for forty years when they came out of Egypt to the Promised Land. Agriculturally, it is the festival of ingathering, a celebration of the fall harvest. *Sukkot* means *booth* and refers to the lean-tos that we are commanded to use as dwellings that we live in during this holiday in memory of the wandering. The celebration should be coming up in a couple of weeks, and it truly is a joyous occasion. The celebration lasts for seven days, and no work is permitted for the first two days. I will be celebrating with the sisters' families. The lean-tos are already under construction. The men are all in the spirit of tabernacling, but the sisters want all the built-in comforts they can get.

Manlius then offered Nicholaus some food and drink and a time of small talk and fellowship followed.

My Teachings Are Not Mine

Nicodemus had a surprise for Nicholaus. He sat himself down, helping himself to some bread and cheese and handed Nicholaus a scroll. "I know that you are keeping copies of the scrolls you are passing on to us, so I thought you might be interested in this one.

Nicholaus paused in his surprise; he then unrolled the scroll and began to read.

Paulus I

May the High Holy One of Israel prosper you and bless you with long life.

I, Saul Ben-Paulus, a Hebrew of Hebrews of the tribe of Benjamin and a Pharisee of Pharisees, am reporting on the assignment I received along with others to patrol the court of the Gentiles, seeking out the false prophet from Nazareth.

For the first three days of the festival, he was nowhere to be found. On the fourth day, we found him teaching in the temple, and we could not help but marvel, saying, "How does this one know letters not being taught."

Jesus answered us, "My teaching is not mine but of the one who sent me. If anyone desires to do his will, he will know concerning the teaching, whether it is of God or I speak from myself. The one speaking from himself seeks his own glory, but the one seeking the glory of the one who sent him, this one is true, and unrighteousness is not in him. Has not Moses given you the law and not one of you does the law? Why do you lust to kill me?"

In the crowd answered, "You have a demon who lusts to kill you?"

Jesus answered, "I did one work, and you all marveled. Because of this, Moses has given you circumcision. Not that it is of Moses but of the Father's. And on the Sabbath, you circumcise a man. If a man receives circumcision on the Sabbath so that the Law of Moses is not broken, are you angry with me because I made a man entirely sound on the Sabbath? Do not judge according to sight but judge righteous judgment." [John 7:14–24 from the Greek]

I have nothing more to report at this time.

The Lord bless you and keep you. The Lord makes His face to shine upon you and be gracious to you. The Lord lift up his countenance upon you and give you peace. [Num. 6:24–26 from the Hebrew]

Nicholaus pondered the contents of this scroll and then remarked, "All they see is a Sabbath violation, and they missed the significance of the healing as a sign of the presence of the Holy Spirit. That gives us further understanding in what Jesus said when you went to interview him about 'birth from above.'" He then labeled the scroll as "Council I" and set it aside.

*****

Later that afternoon, Nicholaus, Levi, and Daniel were busy working when Lady gave out a low quiet bark. Nicholaus looked up from his work to see Ben-Gamaliel approaching his table. He glanced over at Levi and then stood to give a Neeman's greeting to his Pharisee visitor.

Levi understood the situation and took up a new parchment to prepare himself to record the conversation between Ben-Gamaliel and his master.

Ben-Gamaliel turned down the invitation for refreshment and went right to the point. "I have come to seek your opinion concerning the Nazarene teacher and our friend Ben-Gorion. Let me explain.

Levi prepared to write.

Council I

We had people in the temple, and they saw the Nazarene. They said amongst themselves, "Is this not the one they are seeking to kill? And behold, he speaks publicly, and they say nothing to him. Perhaps the rulers truly knew that this is indeed the Christ. But we know this one from where he is. But when the Christ comes, no one knows from where he is."

Jesus therefore cried in the Temple teaching and saying: "Ye both know me, and know whence I am; and I am not come of myself, but He that sent me is true, whom ye know not, I know Him; because I am from Him and He sent me."

They sought therefore to take him, but no man could lay his hands on him. But of the multitude, many believed him, and they said, "When the Christ shall come, will he do more signs than those which this man has done?"

The Pharisees present heard the multitude murmuring these things concerning him, and the chief priests and the Pharisees sent officers to take him.

Jesus therefore said, "Yet a little while, I am with you, and I go on to him that sent me. You shall seek me and shall not find me; and where I am, you cannot come."

The Jews therefore set amongst themselves, "Whither will this man go that we shall not find him? Will he go into the dispersion among the Greeks and teach the Greeks? What is this word that he said, 'Ye shall seek me and shall not find me, and where I am, you cannot come?'" [John 7:25–36 from the Greek]

On the last day, some of the multitude, when they heard him speak, said, "This is truly the prophet." Others said, "This is the Christ." But others said, "No! For does the Christ come out of Galilee? Has not the Scriptures said that the Christ come up out of the seed of David and from Bethlehem, the village where David was?" So there arose a division in the multitude because of him. And some of them would have taken him, but no man laid hands on him.

The officers therefore came to the chief priests and the Pharisees, and they said unto them, "Why did you not bring him?"

The officers answered, "Never, man so spake."

The Pharisees therefore answered them, "Are you also led astray? Have any of the rulers believed on him or the Pharisees? But this multitude, which not knowing the law are accursed."

Ben-Gorion then said onto them, "Does our law judge a man except it first hear from himself and no what he doeth?"

They answered and said onto him, "Art thou also of Galilee? Search and see that out of Galilee arises no prophet. [John 7:40–52 from the Greek]

"Now then, what is your evaluation of the Nazarene and of Ben-Gorion's involvement with him?"

Nicholaus paused for a few moments to consider his answer. "Is the Nazarene the Messiah? My answer is yes and no. I am not convinced that he is the Messiah, the physical warrior king that will rise up a Maccabean-type army and drive the Romans out of Israel. Yes, I am satisfied that he has been sent by the High Holy One to establish a spiritual kingdom here amongst us. This is not a physical world, but one of the Spirit.

"As for Ben-Gorion, he is not the man you first sent to me so many months ago. He now not only accepts me as a Neeman, but he has also become my friend. I find him to be a thorough, dedicated investigator, who is a fervent upkeeper of the law. Is he a follower of the Nazarene? I would have to say yes, to the degree that any investigator follows that which is being investigated."

Ben-Gamaliel spent some time in silence and then promptly excused himself and quickly departed.

Nicholaus looked over to Levi and asked him if he got all that.

Levi said that he did and that he was going to label it "Council II."

She Was Not Condemned

Nicholaus came in at about his usual time for the Sabbath and was surprised to see Levi already at his table working. He asked about Eglah's going to the temple alone. Levi explained that today was her day off so she had the whole day to herself. She had gotten up early and left the baby with Zilpah so she could to go to temple. She wanted to see the Nazarene. He also said that Manlius had promised to keep an eye out for her as he and his detail had temple duty today.

Meanwhile, the girls were on the third floor engaging in their usual girl talk when Cozbi let it be known that she would be happy to find a way to get away from the stigma and drudgery of the third floor and find a good man.

"What's wrong with working up here?" Baara asked. "Eglah has never asked us to do something she doesn't do herself. We have plenty to eat, clothes on our backs, and a warm bed to sleep in. And besides all that, Mistress Abishag has always looked out for our best interest, and she has never asked us to service one of the men."

"Yes, I know. We have it better than we did on the streets, but I want a man to take me away to live in one of those big houses in the upper city. I want to be rid of all this. I want rich food, fine clothes, and servants to do my bidding. Besides, I have been using the street boys to feed myself and give me my needs since as far back as I can remember. I know there is something out there better than this, and I want it."

*****

Work continued for Nicholaus and Levi until midmorning when they were interrupted by Nicodemus making another unscheduled call. He was doing this more often in an attempt to get away from the hubbub of the council and their obsession with the Nazarene. He helped himself to some wine, bread, and cheese as did Nicholaus, who welcomed the midmorning break.

*****

A little later Eglah abruptly entered into Beth Eden. She rushed up out of breath and seated herself at Levi's table and began to regain her composure. She was followed by Manlius, who also joined into the gathering.

Lady jumped up to greet her friends. Eglah cuddled Lady's head in her lap and then exclaimed, "I saw him. In the temple. I saw him." She explained in all her excitement. "All the people came to him, and he taught us. And the scribes and the Pharisees brought to him a woman having been taken in adultery.

"Standing her in the middle, they said to him, 'Teacher, this woman was taken in the very act of committing adultery. The Law of Moses gives us commandment that such should be stoned. You then, what do you say?'

"Bending down, he wrote with his finger in the earth. They continued questioning him. Standing back up, he said to them, 'He that is without sin among you, let him cast the first stone at her.' And bending down again, he wrote on the earth. Hearing this, they went out one by one, beginning from the older ones until the last, and Jesus and the woman were left alone still.

"And Jesus stood back up, and having seen no one but the woman, he said to her, 'Woman, where are those who accused you? Did not one give judgment against you?' And she said, 'No one,

Lord.' And he said to her, 'Neither do I give judgment. Go and sin no more.'" [John 8:2–11 from the Greek]

Eglah could not contain her excitement. "She was not condemned! She was not condemned. And he told her to go and sin no more. His compassion for her is beyond my understanding, and his demonstrated power over the scribes and Pharisees is amazing." With that, Eglah had completed her report and just looked at the men as if waiting for a reply while Levi was busy writing down everything she had said.

Manlius was the first to speak up. "It was a good thing he did what he did because if he had condemned her and they stoned her at his command, I would've had to have him arrested for violating the Roman law. Only a Roman can condemn someone to death and in this case, only the governor."

"It's recorded twice in the books of Moses that both the adulterer and the adulteress should be put to death. I don't understand why the man wasn't brought along with the woman," Nicodemus wondered out loud. "Could it be that he was a fellow Pharisee?"

Nicholaus then commented that it was probably a test to trap the Nazarene so they could bring charges against him for failing to follow the law or for condemning illegally.

The discussion continued for a while until the subject was all talked out.

Eglah excused herself to go home and get her baby, and Manlius returned to his detail.

The men continued their apparent unending discussions of the finer ramifications of the law while Levi was busy finishing writing in a scroll what Eglah had reported. He labeled a new scroll as "Eglah I" and then followed the conversation concerning this recent event.

Late that afternoon, Nicholaus and Levi wrapped up the materials and took them to the security room. Then each of them went their separate ways. Nicholaus headed across the street, with Lady taking the lead.

Nicholaus was surprised at all the commotion he witnessed as he entered the building. Rizpah, a servant girl, ran up to Nicholaus with a basin of water to wash his feet. "What is all the commotion about?" he asked.

Rizpah had a big smile on her face and answered that Sheva was roasting a fatted calf and that the whole neighborhood has been invited to a feast.

"Yes, but why are they having a feast?"

"It's Master Chilion, Master Ben-Adon. It's Master Chilion. He was born blind, but now he can see!"

The Feast

The sisters' house across from Beth Eden was reverberating with celebration. All of the commons was coming in, and they were all bringing food and wine to add to the feast. There was a line-up of servant girls washing the feet of everyone who came in and anointing everyone with sweet-smelling oils. By now, everyone in the commons had heard the good news, and they all wanted to know what happened.

Nicholaus was happy to see Levi, Eglah, Daniel, and Zilpah come in. They had been given a special invitation by the sisters, who considered them to be family. They took their assigned places, reclining at the table with Eglah and Zilpah between Levi and Nicholaus and Daniel on Levi's other side.

Nicholaus recognized a group of Pharisees who were in native dress. At times they, like the Romans, would use common native dress to go out in public without drawing attention to their presence. Nicodemus was in the group, as was his friend Joseph. Saul Ben-Paulus and some of his like-minded ultras were also present. Nicholaus did not recognize the rest of them individually but understood what they were by their standoffishness and mannerisms. You can take a Pharisee out of his costume, but you can't get the Pharisee out of the man.

Everyone was talking about the miracle and wanted to hear what had happened to Chilion that he had received his sight. Everyone became quiet when he got up to speak.

"I was at the gate to the temple, as is my habit on the Sabbath. I heard a commotion approaching me, and then I heard someone say, 'Teacher, who sinned, this one or his parents that he was born blind?' This was when I felt they were talking about me. A voice answered, 'Neither this one nor his parents, but that the works of God might be revealed in him. It is necessary for me to work the works of him who sent me while it is day; night comes when no one will be able to work. While I am in the world, I am the light of the world.'

"I was later told that after saying these things, he spat on the ground and made clay out of spittle and anointed clay on my eyes. He then said to me, 'Go, wash in the pool of Siloam', and I went and washed and came away seeing. Later, I was told that the man who made clay and anointed my eyes was Jesus of Nazareth." [John 9:2–7 from the Greek]

The people marveled at the story they were told. Nicholaus looked over at Levi and said, "Use my study. You will find everything you need there." With that, Levi nodded in understanding and excused himself to go to the study to write down what he had just heard.

The feast continued with a buzz of conversations about what was said. The Pharisees were obviously in deep discussion over what they had just heard.

Later, Levi returned to his place and told Nicholaus that he had made two copies and labeled them "Ben-Benaiah I." One was in his chest at the end of his bed, and he had the other one. He would make arrangements to pay him in the morning.

A little later, Nicodemus came up to Nicholaus and asked him to join him and his friends with the rest of the Pharisees. Nicholaus looked at Levi, and Levi nodded his understanding. Nicholaus then excused himself and followed Nicodemus to his table. Levi followed behind and stood along the wall with the other people, where he could hear what was being said.

Nicodemus introduced Nicholaus by saying, "This is my Neeman friend, the mediator, Awnee Ben-Adon. He is the one who has been providing the council with all the Baptist and Nazarene scrolls." Nicodemus then introduced each of the Pharisees to Nicholaus.

There was a brief time of light conversation; then came the question that everyone wanted to ask. "What do you think of what you just heard?"

Nicholaus was surprised by the boldness of the question being given to a Neeman. He paused for a moment and then answered, "In this gathering, what I think is ill relevant. What is most important is what you think. After all, you are the rulers of the Jews."

Ben-Paulus spoke up first, "I see two violations of the law here. The first is healing on the Sabbath, and the second is manufacturing clay on the Sabbath. Both are clearly violations of the Law." This was followed by a lengthy conversation amongst the Pharisees concerning the written law and the verbal laws concerning the keeping of the Sabbath.

Nicholaus finally asked if he could play Beelzebub's scribe* and, with their permission, asked them some questions. Everyone approved.

Nicholaus paused to put his arguments in order and then said, "What is the labor that the law requires us to engage ourselves in for the first six days of the week? What constitutes work?

"I submit to you that work is a physical or mental effort or activity that is a means of livelihood. It is a duty or task to be performed as assigned to them by someone when they are under authority. It is a person's employment or occupation as a means of earning an income, supporting ones family, conducting business, or gleaning a reward.

"On the seventh day, the High Holy One rested from his labors and intended for all of Israel to rest from their labors, along with all in each household be they slave, indentured or free. It was to be a day of rest.

"The Mishnah has turned the day of rest into a day of torment with its excessive dos and don'ts. The herds still need tending, and the flocks still need feeding. He who is in need is still in need of a helping hand. Israel's lamb is lost! Will you help find it?

166

"To say that the Nazarene is working when he heals someone is wrong. The man is not a physician, and he is not receiving an income or reward for his efforts. The man is not a potter. Therefore making clay is not the labor of his occupation, and again, he is receiving no income or reward for his efforts."

"You, on the other hand, never cease working. You are always watching others looking for violations of the law so that you can condemn someone, and you do it for your own self-esteem or to improve your standing amongst your fellow Pharisees. This is gleaning a reward.

"The Nazarene does not fit your definition or description of a good Jew, but who does? If you are honest with yourselves, you will find that even some in your ranks do not measure up to your high standards. Everyone is a prisoner of his own beliefs. No one can eliminate their prejudices. They can just recognize and deal with them." With that, Nicholaus concluded his argument. "I trust you will receive these arguments in the spirit in which they were given. I intended no disrespect to anyone, and I humbly apologize if any was perceived."

Nicodemus then responded, "Your arguments are beyond our teachings but worthy of our consideration."

With this, Nicholaus excused himself and returned to his place with Levi following behind. They both reclined in their places.

"You were a little harsh with the Pharisees," Levi said. "Do I have another scroll to write?"

Nicholaus assured him that he did not. "I'm quite sure that the only record will be the one added to my file in the Office of the Ruling Council of the Pharisees. They have just enough religion to make them hate but not enough to allow them to love. Always remember that if no one ever objects to what you have to say, you are probably not saying anything that matters."

37

The Unborn Sin

Levi, Eglah, and the girls were making their rounds at the market. They had stopped in the shops of Jada Ben-Lahad, the jeweler, and Towb Ben-Rawkal to pay their respects.

Later, Eglah was bartering with a street merchant over the price of some material while Levi was looking at a new supply of ink. Baara saw Cozbi slip a bangle under her robe without paying for it.

*****

Nicodemus was already setting at his table when Nicholaus entered Beth Eden. The Beth Eden servant girls were just making their morning deliveries of bread, fruit, and wine.

With a surprised look on his face, Nicholaus asked, "What brings you out so early this morning?"

Nicodemus smiled and said, "You do. That was quite a hornet's nest you stirred up last night, my friend, with your Beelzebub's scribe arguments. Joseph agreed with you and was the leader of the group that was on your side. Saul Ben-Paulus was the most vocal in his disagreement. The arguing went on for some time. If nothing else, there is a larger group of Pharisees who know who you are and where you stand. You might even have some new customers out of it all. You did well, my friend. You did well."

Nicholaus took his seat, thanking his friend for his commentary, and then produced a scroll from his cloak and handed it to Nicodemus. It was entitled "Ben-Benaiah I," the scroll that Levi had written the night before.

Nicodemus unrolled and read the scroll. "This is well-written. Levi never ceases to amaze me with his ability to remember everything."

At this time, Levi came to his table, shortly followed by Daniel. Levi had picked up that which he needed from the security rooms. The men seated themselves and began their work; Daniel then headed back to the security rooms for something he forgot. Levi was still listening to the conversation at the next table. He knew they were talking about his new scroll, and he prepared himself to take notes.

Nicodemus continued his questioning. "I didn't notice it last night, but now I can't help but take notice of the question his followers asked the Nazarene. 'Who sinned, this man or his parents that he was born blind?' The question begs a discussion of whether or not it is possible for an unborn baby to commit sin. The only way the sin of a man born blind could have been committed by him is if he committed it before he was born."

Nicholaus noted, "Jacob and Esau were fighting in their mother's womb [Genesis 25 from the Hebrew]. And what about Jeremiah, whom God formed in his mother's womb, was he not set apart to be a prophet before he was born? [Jeremiah 1 from the Hebrew]. Samson was also set aside to be a Nazirite [Judges 13:7 from the Hebrew]. If a person can fight with his brother or be set aside to be a prophet or a Nazirite before he is born, can he not also sin?"

At this point, Levi entered into the conversation. "When Eglah was carrying Huldah, she had cravings for strange combinations of foods. She accredited this to Huldah's telling her what she likes and dislikes. Maybe there is something to the question that his followers asked. If a baby can influence its mother's eating habits, maybe it is possible for a baby to sin before it's born."

Nicodemus now spoke up. "The Nazarene accepted the question as it was given. His answer that neither the man nor his parents sinned would further indicate his acceptance of the possibility of an unborn child committing sin."

"What do you think of his statement that 'while he is in the world, he is the light of the world'?"

"The kingdom, the kingdom, it's all about the kingdom," Nicholaus replied. "He is saying that he is a lamp in this world. Casting light upon the kingdom. This is his spiritual kingdom. He's telling us that he is not of this world, but he is of the spirit world. That is the kingdom that both he and the Baptist have been teaching about. And when he told him to wash in the pool of Siloam, he reminded me of Elisha telling Naaman to go and dip himself in the Jordan that he might be cured of his leprosy." [2 Kings 5:10 from the Hebrew]

Nicodemus then asked, "What do you think about his doing the works of God?"

"The man thinks himself to be a prophet as well as a king, and he is declaring that it is not him, but God, who is working these miracles through him."

"Not only can Chilion now see, but his entire being has been changed," Nicodemus said. "It is almost as if he was talking to himself. I knew him from the market and from the gate when he used to sit and beg, but I could hardly recognize him as being the same person last night."

The conversation continued, rehashing what had already been said. The three men had their morning meal together, and then Nicodemus excused himself to take the scroll to the council chambers.

*****

When Eglah and the girls returned to Beth Eden, Baara took Eglah aside and told her what she saw.

Eglah then confronted Cozbi about the bangle. Cozbi said that it was true. She had seen the bangle, and she wanted it.

Eglah gave her a choice. She could return the bangle and apologize, or she would have to leave Beth Eden until she does. The next morning, Cozbi was nowhere to be found.

They Threw Him Out

The following morning, Nicholaus came in at his usual time. Levi was off to the market with Eglah and Baara. Lady curled up comfortably behind his chair. It was relatively quiet, and Nicholaus was enjoying the lack of involvement that was his normal state of affairs. He ate bread and cheese and sipped from his cup, and he sat back to have a quiet time.

Levi came in from his trip to the market and began working on some contracts. He also was enjoying this non-involvement with new opportunities.

Nicholaus made his weekly luncheon date with Mistress Abishag, and it too was a quiet uneventful time of nourishment and comradeship.

But that afternoon brought a change.

Sheva Ben-Benaiah came in with Chilion. "Master Nicholaus, they threw him out of the temple! The Pharisees—they threw him out of the temple. What should we do? What should we do? The first time in his entire life that he could go into the men's court, and they threw him out of the temple!"

"Sit down and relax for a minute, and then tell me what happened."

Levi unrolled a new scroll and began to record what Chilion was about to say.

Ben-Benaiah II

This morning I went back to where I used to sit and beg. Some of the people recognized me, but others were not sure. Then I told them that I am he. Then they said to me, "How were your eyes opened?"

I answered and said: "A man called Jesus made clay and anointed my eyes and told me to go to the pool of Siloam and wash." and going and washing, I received my sight.

Then they said to me, "Where is that one?"

I told them that I did not know.

They then brought me to the Pharisees, and it was a Sabbath when Jesus made the clay and opened my eyes.

The Pharisees again asked me. How I had received my sight, and I told them that he put clay on my eyes and I washed, and I see.

Then some of the Pharisees said that this man is not from God because he does not keep the Sabbath. Others said how can a man, a sinner, do such miracles? And there was division among them.

They then said to me, "What do you say about him, because he opened your eyes?"

And I said that he is a prophet.

They did not believe me, and they called my parents, and they asked them if I was their son whom they said was born blind. They then asked, "How does he now see?"

My parents answered and said that "We know this is our son and that he was born blind. But how he now sees, we do not know nor who opened his eyes we do not know. He is of age. Ask him. He will speak about this for himself."

Then a second time, they called me and said: "Give glory to God. We know that this man is the sinner."

Then I answered them, saying: "Whether he is a sinner or not, I do not know. One thing I do know that being blind, I now see."

And they said to me again, "What did he do to you? How did he open your eyes?"

I answered them that "I told them already, and you did not hear? Why do you wish to hear again? Do you also desire to become a disciple of him?"

Then they reviled me and said that "You are a disciple of that one. But we are disciples of Moses. We know that God spoke by Moses, but this one, we do not know from whence he is."

I then asked them, "From where is the marvel in this that you do not know from where he is and he opened my eyes?"

"But we know that God does not hear sinful ones. But if anyone is God fearing and does His will, He hears that one."

Never was it ever heard that anyone opened the eyes of one having been born blind. If this one was not from God, He could not do anything. They then told me that I was born wholly in sin. And do I teach them? And they threw me out. [John 9:8–34 from the Greek]

"You are okay. It takes a pronouncement and assembly of ten or more in the synagogue and a formal trial for them to cast you out of the synagogue. Give it some time, and you will be able to go back with no problems.

The conversation continued for a while, and then Ben-Benaiah and Chilion excused themselves and departed.

Levi said that he had recorded the conversation and labeled it "Ben-Benaiah II." Then he said that he would make another copy for the council.

Nicholaus thought about this for a moment and then told Levi to forget about giving the council a copy of this one, but they would add it to the scrolls in the locked chest at the foot of his bed.

Do You Believe?

L evi was involved with a great number of contracts that had all come in at once, so Daniel had the job of escorting Eglah and Baara to the market.

Daniel was being most attentive to everything that was going on, engaging in more conversation then Levi ever did. Eglah thought the extra attention was refreshing; Baara thought it was charming. When they arrived back at Beth Eden, the girls ran upstairs, packages in hand, giggling all the way.

Daniel went directly to his table, where he had a pile of work to do. Lady got up to greet her new friend and then lay back down.

*****

At Beth Eden, it was relatively quiet with one exception. Jada Ben-Lahad, the jeweler, who came to visit Levi and Daniel. Marcus Manlius came to visit Nicholaus. All three had the same question; they wanted to know what had happened to Chilion.

Each of them told their story and answered all the questions that were being asked by their visitors. This was just the beginning. From time to time, others came in and wanted to hear the story also. Each of the men was patient with his guests and answered all of their questions.

When they went for their midday meal, Lady ran on ahead as she always did. She knew she had a dish waiting for her in the kitchen. Nicholaus took the lead, followed by Levi and then Daniel. The pecking order had been well established.

Levi could not help but notice that Nicholaus was leaning on his staff much more than he normally did, and he was a little slower climbing the stairs. Levi asked him if he was all right and if his legs hurt.

"No, but they are getting stiff with old age."

As the three took their places, even the servant girls wanted to know what had happened, so they explained it all over again. When their meals came, they were finally able to enjoy them in peace and quiet.

*****

Later that afternoon, the three men decided that they would close shop early and hoped that they might be able to get more work done on the following day.

Nicholaus went across the street while Levi and Daniel cleaned up the tables and took everything to the security rooms.

Nicholaus was happy to once again be at home. Rizpah, the servant girl, met him at the door to wash his feet. It was early, so he retired to his study to relax and then refreshed himself for dinner. The evening meal was excellent as it usually was. The small talk was congenial, and Nicholaus was content to spend this time with those he considered to be his friends and family.

When the family evening meal was over, the men retired to the roof for their evening cup of wine and conversation.

Chilion started the conversation by stating that he had had another encounter with the Nazarene. He said that "Jesus came to me and said, 'Do you believe in the Son of God?'"

"I answered Him and asked, 'Who is he, Lord, that I might believe in him?'"

"And Jesus said, 'You have both seen him and it is he speaking with you who is that one.'"

"I believe, Lord!" And I worshiped him."

"And Jesus said, 'I came into this world for judgment that the ones who do not see may see and they who see may become blind.'"

"The Pharisees who were with me heard this and said to him, 'Are we also blind?'"

"And Jesus said to them: 'If you were blind, you would have no sin. But now you say, we see. Therefore your sin remains.'" [John 9:35–41 from the Greek]

"Tell me, Master Ben-Adon, why are the Pharisees so close-minded to that which has happened? Why can't they accept that Jesus has cured my blindness and made me to see?"

"You, my friend, have challenged their core beliefs. Their traditions are strong, and to change from that tradition is hard. A Pharisee of Pharisees has spent his entire life being saturated with their family traditions and that of their movement to keep the law. For them, the teachings of the ages are beyond reproach, and anything contrary to that teaching is evil and sinful. Their only experience is that of keeping the law as they have been taught the law, and for them, it would be a sin to deviate from it.

"Your experience is that 'Once you were blind but now you see,' and your experience teaches you that Jesus the Nazarene is the one who caused you to see. Your experience and your reason have brought you to believe that he is the Messiah, the Son of God, the one to be worshiped. As Jesus said, your eyes have been opened, that is your spiritual eyes as well as your physical ones."

"Your sins have been forgiven, and you are now on the threshold of the kingdom of God, that spirit world that is all around this physical world that we live in."

After a period of small talk, the men retired for the evening. Nicholaus went to his study and recorded what Chilion had said. He labeled it Ben-Benaiah III and stored it away in the locked chest at the foot of his bed.

Dreams?

Weeks had gone by with no reports about the Nazarene. Speculation is that he has returned to Galilee and that the people up there have lost interest in sending reports.

Nicodemus made his usual weekly stop and settled down for a leisure morning meal and fellowship with his friend Nicholaus.

Manlius came to the table and joined in on the leisure conversation.

A little later, the three of them were joined by a fourth. It was Ahikar Bar-Jathan from Cana of Galilee. "I have a new scroll for you. It comes to you from Nathaniel Bar-Tholomew—well, actually from his mother. She reported to me that this is a story given to her by her son, and I thought it worthy of reporting to you." With this, he handed Nicholaus a scroll. Nicholaus unrolled and briefly read it, and then he handed it to Levi.

About now, Lady was laying on her side kicking her legs and grunting.

Bar-Jathan asked, "What is wrong with your dog?"

"Oh nothing, she's just dreaming. She's probably chasing a cat somewhere. She does this at times. It's nothing to worry about."

Manlius then remarked, "Another worshiper of the Greek god Morpheus."

"Who is Morpheus?" Bar-Jathan asked.

"Morpheus was the Greek god of dreams, of warnings and of prophecies, for those who slept in his temples or shrines. He was alleged to bring messages from the gods to rulers of kingdoms and the commanders of armies. I don't put much stock in it myself, but there are those in our command who do."

Nicholaus spoke, "To the Jew, dreams are considered part of life's natural experiences. There are those who believe that lessons can be garnered from their interpretations. The ancient Hebrews considered dreams to be the voice of the High Holy One. Good dreams came from him, and bad ones came from evil spirits. The prophet Samuel would lie down to sleep in the temple before the Ark of the Covenant to receive word from the Lord."

Nicodemus then added, "The Greek, Antipon, wrote a book about dreams centuries ago. Hippocrates had a theory that during the day, the soul receives images. During the night, it produces those images as dreams. Aristotle, on the other hand thought dreams could analyze illnesses and predict diseases. There are many theories, but one is hard-pressed to be able to prove any of them."

Bar-Jathan then said that a number of scrolls are available about dreams and their interpretations.

"Scrolls had been written on the subject, it is true, but quite frankly, I believe they're nothing more than a bunch of camel dung," Nicholaus offered. "Dreams are nothing more than your brain doing its nightly house cleaning, and the interpretation of dreams is nothing more than a charlatan's money-making scheme."

Manlius then added the observation that everywhere Rome went, the people dreamed of independence but adjusted to their presence and for keeping of Roman law.

Nicholaus replied that brute power can conquer and control a people, but it can't win the peace?

The idle conversation continued until it was nearly time for their midday meals. Eventually each of the visitors excused himself and went his separate way.

*****

Nicholaus made his weekly luncheon date with Mistress Abishag, but there was a present addition to the gathering. Levi, Eglah, Daniel, and Baara joined in.

The luncheon was progressing with the normal small talk between the parties. Eglah then asked, "What is your secret, Master Nicholaus? What do you accredit for your many great success?"

"Three things: my faith in God, my father's teachings, and a lifetime of experiences. From as far back as I can remember I have always paid my tithes to the synagogue and or some worthy ministry, along with my offerings and almsgiving. I consider this as the most important of all. To not pay your tithe is robbing God, and it will bring God's curse upon you by withdrawing himself from you. On the other hand, paying your tithes will cause God to open the windows of heaven for you and pour out his blessing upon you. God also promises to rebuke the devourer for you, if you pay your tithes." [Malachi 3:8–10 from the Hebrew] "Also, it is recorded in the Scroll of Proverbs that we should trust in the Lord with all of our hearts, and lean not on our own understanding. In all our ways acknowledge him, and he will direct our paths. [Prov. 3:5–6 from the Hebrew]

"My father taught me to always treat people honestly and fairly. Never expect more than they can give and never give less then you're capable of giving. There are those that would say that this is a poor business practice, but I have found over the years that it is the best of advice."

Later Mistress Abishag said, "Tell us about the writers of your scrolls. What motivates them, and can you trust everything that they should write?"

"The first motivating factor is money. They are well paid for their contributions. The second motivator is their loyalty to the movement. Second, third- and fourth-generation Pharisees have lived for the cause all their lives. And to them, a request from the Council of Ruling Elders is likened onto a request from God. As to their trustworthiness, the third is their own curiosity.

"I have found that what they submit is truthful. But they don't always tell the whole truth. Sometimes their preconceived opinions cloud their ability to report. Others report only what they believe the council will be pleased to hear and some only what is in agreement with their ideas of what is probably the situation. The irregularities in their reports soon become apparent and are taken under consideration accordingly."

"What do you do when there are irregularities?" Eglah asked.

"I just point them out and let the council deal with them."

The luncheon went longer than normal but was greatly enjoyed by all. Eventually it broke up, and each went their separate ways.

The Seventy

Nicodemus was anxious to read the new scroll that came down from Cana. He was starting to lose faith in the Council at Sepphoris and their ability to motivate their people in Galilee to send down reports. Bar-Jathan's report from Bar-Tholomew was encouraging and of most interest. Any report of the inner workings of the followers of the Nazarene was of great interest to the Council of Ruling Elders.

Upon entering Beth Eden, he quickly took his place with Nicholaus and poured himself a cup of wine. "Is the scroll ready?" he asked.

Nicholaus had a smile on his face as he pawed his way through the scrolls that were on his desk. He paused for a moment, and then he reached over on Levi's desk and retrieved the scroll he was looking for. He checked it over and then handed it to Nicodemus, who quickly unrolled it and begin to read.

Nathanael III

Greetings in the name of the High Holy One of Israel. May His blessing be upon you and yours, and may he bring peace to Jerusalem and all of Israel.

I, Ahikar Bar-Jathan, from Cana, am the writer of this account as it was given to me by Nathanael Bar-Tholomew.

The Lord also appointed seventy others, not of the disciples, and set them two by two before his face into every city and place where he was about to come.

Then he said to them, "Indeed, the harvest is much, but the laborers are few. Therefore, pray to the Lord of the harvest that he send out workers into his harvest. Go. Behold, I send you out as lambs in the midst of wolves. Do not carry a purse, nor a moneybag nor sandals and greet no one along the way.

"And into whatever house you may enter, first say, 'Peace to this house.' And if a son of peace is truly there, your peace shall rest on it. But if not so, it shall return to you. And remain in the same house, eating and drinking the things shared by them, for the laborer is worthy of his higher. Do not move from house to house. And into whatever city you are and they receive you, eat the things set before you. And heal the sick in it and say to them, "The kingdom of God has drawn near to you.

"But into whatever city you enter and they do not receive you, having gone out into the street, say, 'Even the dust which clings to us out of your city, we wipe off against you! Yet know this, the Kingdom of God has drawn near to you!'" [Luke 10:1–11 from the Greek]

I have nothing more to report at this time, but I did find this report to be very interesting and worthy of the attention of the Council of Ruling Elders.

The Lord bless you and keep you. The Lord make His face to shine upon you and be gracious to you. The Lord lift up his countenance upon you and give you peace. [Num. 6:24–26 from the Hebrew]

"He sent out seventy. His ministry is growing."

"Yes, but did you notice? 'The harvest is much, but the laborers are few.' And what about 'Heal the sick and say to them, "The kingdom of God has drawn near to you.' He gave to the seventy the ability to save the sick."

"Yes. We will be interested to read a follow-up report to see what and how they did."

*****

Later that day, Levi and Daniel were off to see Ben-Lahad, the jeweler, about some contracts but more probably to shop and to have some leisure time together. Nicholaus understood and really didn't mind.

Judah Ben-Penuel came in followed by Eglah with the baby, which demanded the immediate attention of Lady. She placed the baby on Levi's table, and Lady jumped up in the Levi's chair to watch over her. Eglah then sat down at the Levi's table.

Ben-Penuel, who is a courier from the High Council in Sepphoris, went straight to Nicholaus and presented him with a scroll. "This was sent to us for our information, and now the Council has sent it down to you."

Nicholaus stood to greet his guest. "Thank you, my friend. Can you stay for a while?"

"No. I must run, I have many more chores to do before I go back to Sepphoris." With that, Nicholaus paid him, and he left.

Eglah then moved over to the other table with Nicholaus and stated that she had a question for him. "Last night, I looked up the passage you were talking about in Malachi, and I don't understand how the devourer would be relevant to Levi and me? We do not have fields or vines. How would this apply to us?"

"As I understand, the devourer is an evil spiritual personality and one of Beelzebub's servants. He comes in many forms. Basically, his job is to take away everything that he can. Understand that everything belongs to God, and everything that we have is a gift from God. In return, God asked that we pay a tithe that is ten percent on everything he gives us back to him for his ministry. The Pharisees put much stock in temporal promises and serve God with the intent of a reward. Those of us who keep the word and pay our tithes, along with our offerings and almsgiving, do not necessarily become rich, but we never lack for our needs.

"The devourer, on the other hand, will consume one's riches by enticing him with meaningless expensive habits and pastimes. You can see the results of his endeavors all around us. There are those who take pride in any or everything other than pleasing God. These and many more are the results of the endeavors of the devourer."

"I think I am starting to understand why Levi has always insisted on paying tithe and making offerings. Thank you for your explanation. Levi is always talking about your rules, but he never told me what they were. Can you tell me?"

"I have three rules and three exceptions to the rules. The rules are one, always do for others what you would have them do for you; two, do for yourself what you would do for others; and three, do not do for others what they can do for themselves. The exceptions are the egotists, bullies, and despots. I have no use whatsoever for those three personalities."

"Thank you for that explanation. Those sound like good rules, and I understand and agree with your exceptions. I always enjoy talking with you. You always seem to be able to make the most complicated simple and plain. Thank you."

With this, Eglah gathered up the baby, patted Lady on the head, telling her how good a dog she was, and then left the building.

The Good Samaritan

L evi felt like a second left foot. Eglah and Baara were chattering away like he wasn't even there. They were going from stall to stall, looking at everything. On and on they went, and Levi couldn't help but think that they were taking way too much time.

*****

Nicodemus came wandering in well past his usual hour. To his surprise, Nicholaus and Levi were both missing. Daniel was at his table working, so Nicodemus went to his table and sat down. "Where is everybody?" he asked.

Daniel jumped up trembling and answered, "Master Nicholaus has not come in yet, and Master Levi is escorting his wife and Baara at the market. Is there something I can do for you? Please, seat yourself at the master's table and help yourself to the food and drink. I'm sure that Master would be pleased if you were to do so."

Nicodemus was surprised to hear someone call Levi "Master," but all things considered, it seemed appropriate, he stayed in his seat and passed up the food and drink. *"It just wouldn't be proper without my friend."* He thought to himself, and then he said, "Thank you. No. I'll be comfortable here. Do you know if there are any scrolls for me?"

"Yes. There is one. I just finished working on it last night. Here, let me find it for you." With that, Daniel looked through some scrolls on his table, sorted out one, and handed it to Nicodemus.

Nicodemus was surprised to hear that Daniel was now working on scrolls. He would have to look at this one with a more critical eye, he thought to himself. He opened the scroll and began to read.

Galilean XVI

Greetings in the name of Jehovah, the High Holy One of Israel. I am Joseph Bar-Lecah, a Pharisee of the tribe of Judah.

A scribe stood up in the synagogue and asked the Nazarene, "Master, what shall I do that I may inherit eternal life?"

"What has been written in the law? How do you read it?"

And answering, he said, "You shall love the High Holy One with all your heart and with all your soul and with all your strength and with all your mind, and your neighbor as yourself."

"You have answered rightly, do this and you shall live."

"And who is my neighbor?"

Jesus replied to the scribe, "A certain man was going down from Jerusalem to Jericho, and fell amongst robbers, who both stripped him and laid on the wounds. Going away, they left him being half-dead. But by coincidence, a certain priest went down on that road, and seeing him, he passed on the opposite side. And in the same way, a Levite also being at the place coming and seeing him, he passed on the opposite side. But a certain Samaritan came upon him and seeing him, he was filled with pity. And coming near, he bound up his wounds and poured on oil and wine. And putting him on his own animal, he brought him to an inn and cared for him. And going forth on the next day, he took out two denarii. He gave them to the innkeeper and said to him, "Care for him, and whatever more you spend, I, on my return, will repay you."

Continuing his answer, Jesus said, "Who then of these three seems to you to have become a neighbor to the one having fallen amongst robbers?"

"The one having done the deed of mercy with him."

Then the Nazarene said to him, "Go and you do likewise." [Luke 10:25–37 from the Greek]

I find this answer to be insulting to priests and Levites, and I think the Nazarene needs to learn his place in life.

The Lord bless you and keep you. The Lord make His face to shine upon you and be gracious to you. The Lord lift up his countenance upon you and give you peace. [Num. 6:24–26 from the Hebrew]

Nicodemus was impressed. "You did a good job on this scroll." With that, he paid Daniel and got up to go, just as Nicholaus came in.

Nicodemus gave his friend a proper greeting and then asked, "Where were you? I was beginning to worry about you, my friend."

"I wasn't feeling good this morning, so I took my time and waited for the discomforts to pass before coming to work."

"So tell me, what seemed to be the problem?"

"I don't know. My chest felt like there was a heavy weight on it. I was taking short shallow breaths, and I had the cold sweats. After a while, it all passed, and I felt fine, so I came into work."

"Have you seen a doctor?"

"No. Everything went away, and I am just fine now. Seeing a doctor would just be a waste of his time and my money. I'll be all right. I'm just going to have to take it easy for the next few days. Tell me, did Daniel take care of you all right?"

"Daniel was the perfect host. He gave me the Samaritan scroll, and I was just ready to go when you came in."

The conversation was then reduced to idle conversation as the two friends enjoyed each other's company.

A Crippled Woman

Nicodemus was late again. Nicholaus was up to his neck in negotiations with two merchants, but he was still beginning to wonder if his friend was coming in at all. Daniel was already back from the market and working at his table.

Nicodemus finally came in only to find that someone else was in his chair. The other chair was occupied as well. *That is what I get for going to the secretary's office first*, he thought. The men at Nicholaus's table were having a heated discussion over the finer points of their deal, and Nicholaus was trying to find a common ground for them.

Levi was not at his table, so Nicodemus took a seat at Daniel's table and asked, "How long has this been going on?"

Daniel said that he was not sure as they were there when he came in.

The men engaged in small talk about the weather and business in general until Nicholaus's guests resolved their differences and left the building together.

Nicodemus excused himself from Daniel and joined his friend at his table. "I went to the secretary's office this morning and was trapped in with a discussion about the Nazarene, his followers, and the preparations for Passover. This obsession with the Passover is distracting everyone. They have a Planning Committee. I don't understand why they don't just leave them alone and let the committee do its work."

"I have learned a long time ago, if you really want something done right, don't give it to a committee. This might cheer you up: there is another scroll down from Galilee."

Nicodemus took the scroll handed to him and began to read.

Bar-Lecah I

I was passing through Judah and stopped in a synagogue on the Sabbath. There was a woman there having a spirit of infirmity for eighteen years and was bent together and was not able to completely stand up.

The Nazarene called her near and said to her, "Woman, you have been set free from your infirmity." And he laid hands on her, and instantly she was made erect and glorified God.

This made the synagogue ruler angry that Jesus healed on the Sabbath. He said to the crowd, "There are six days in which it is right to work. Therefore coming in these, be healed, and not on the Sabbath day."

The Nazarene answered him and said, "Hypocrite! Each one of you on the Sabbath. Does he not untie his ox or his ass from the manger and lead it away to give a drink? And this one being a daughter of Abraham whom Satan has bound low for eighteen years, ought she not to be healed from this bond on the Sabbath Day?"

On his saying these things, all who were opposed to him were ashamed. And all the crowd rejoiced over all the glorious things taking place by him. [Luke 13:10–17 from the Greek]

The Lord bless you and keep you. The Lord make His face to shine upon you and be gracious to you. The Lord lift up his countenance upon

you and give you peace. [Num. 6:24–26 from
the Hebrew]

Nicodemus, as if thinking out loud, exclaimed, "She was having
a spirit of infirmity for eighteen years. Is he telling us that an eigh-
teen-year physical infirmity was being caused by a spirit? And his
argument about the ox and the ass are factual. It reminds me of your
Beelzebub's scribe arguments. This scroll causes more questions than
it gives answers. Oh, by the way, I have one for your collection. It is a
report from Ben-Paulus. With that, he removed a scroll from his robe
and handed it to Nicholaus.

Ben-Paulus II

In response to a request from the elders, I,
Saul Ben-Paulus, was in the temple, and I saw
the Nazarene walking in the temple in Solomon's
porch. A group of us Pharisees encircled him and
said to him, "How long do you lift up our soul?
If you are the Christ, tell us publicly."

The Nazarene answered them, saying: "I
told you, and you did not believe. The works
which I do in the name of my Father, these bear
witness about me. But you do not believe, for
you are not of my sheep. As I said to you, my
sheep hear my voice and I know them and they
follow me and I give eternal life to them and they
shall never, ever perish, and not anyone shall
pluck them out of my hand. My Father, who has
given them to me, is greater than all. And no one
is able to pluck them out of my Father's hand. I
and the Father are one!"

Then the Pharisees again took up stones
that they might stone him.

Jesus answered them, "I showed you many
good works from my Father. For which works of
them do you stone me?"

The Jews answered him, saying: "We do not stone you concerning a good work but concerning blasphemy and because you, being a man, make yourself a God."

"Is it not written in your Law, 'I said you are gods'? If he called those gods which whom the word of God was and Scripture cannot be broken, do you say to him whom the Father sanctified and sent into the world. You blaspheme because I said I am the Son of God? If I do not do the works of my Father, do not believe me. But if I do, even if you do not believe me, believe the works that you may perceive and believe that the Father is in me and I am in him."

Then they again sought to seize him, and he went forth out of their hand. [John 10:23–39 from the Greek]

"'I and the Father are one!' He most definitely considers himself to be the Messiah, and he is not making any excuses for it. This is a 'take it or leave it' declaration. There is no middle ground. Believe and be a part of his spiritual kingdom, or don't believe and you are not."

Nicodemus smiles, and the conversation continues.

Lazarus

Joseph Ben-Caiaphas was in his study, trying to enjoy his morning time of meditation and prayer. Jabin Ben-Geber, his first secretary, came in. Caiaphas knew the footfall of his secretary, and he didn't have to look up to know who was interrupting his private time.

"Excuse me for interrupting your prayers, but we must talk about Passover. The Planning Committee needs to know which direction they are to go this year. Can they have the Court of the Gentiles back, or do they have to use the upper market, the theater, and the hippodrome again. Time is running out for them, and they need a decision."

Caiaphas was annoyed by the question, but he chose to discuss it anyway. *Running out of time? Time is all they have*, he thought to himself. Out loud, he said, "We lost money again last year. The Nazarene and his followers never showed up, and security was spread too thin trying to cover three locations all at the same time, and everybody complained about the new arrangements." He paused to ponder the situation and then he said, "Bring them all back into the temple."

"As you wish," Ben-Geber responded. He excused himself and backed out of the presence of his master.

*****

The next day, Nicodemus came in shaking his head and slumped down into his usual chair. "They did it to us again. Just like two years ago. They are kicking us out of the Court of the Gentiles in favor vendors and moneychangers again. I'm going to have to find someplace else to teach my students. I don't know when this is all going to end. There is just no justice in it all."

Nicholaus sympathized with his friend and thought to himself that he had a table in Beth Eden that the priests would never want. "Maybe this will cheer you up and put that old spring back in your step." With that, Nicholaus gave him a new scroll.

With a smile on his face, Nicodemus unrolled the scroll and began to read.

Bethany I

I, Athaliah, am the widow of Simon Ben-Judah, who was a member of your Council of Ruling Elders. I am aware of the inquiries you have made concerning the Rabbi, Jesus of Nazareth.

I was in the home of Mary and Martha here in Bethany comforting them because Lazarus, their brother, had died.

On the fourth day, I saw Mary quickly rise up and go out. I followed her saying she is going to the tomb so that she may weep there. Then she came to where Jesus was, and seeing him, she fell down at his feet, saying to him, "Lord, if you were here, my brother would not have died."

Then when he saw her weeping and the Jews who came down with her weeping, Jesus groaned in the spirit and troubled himself. And he said, "Where have you put him?"

We answered, "Look, come and see."

Jesus wept.

Then the Jews said, "See how he loved him."

But some of them said, "Was this one, the one opening the eyes of the blind, not able to have caused that this one should not have died?"

Jesus came to the tomb, which was a cave, and there was a stone lying over the entrance. Jesus said, "Take away the stone."

Martha then said to him, "Lord, he already smells, for it is the fourth day."

Jesus then said to her, "Did I not say to you that if you would believe you will see the glory of God?"

We then took away the stone where the dead one was laid. Jesus lifted his eyes upward and said, "Father, I thank you that you heard me. And I know that you always hear me, but because of the crowd who stand around, I say it that they might believe that you sent me." And saying these things, he cried out with a loud voice, "Lazarus! Come outside!"

And the one who had died came out, having his feet and hands bound with sheets and his face being bound with a cloth. Jesus said to them, "untie him and let him go." Then many of us, those coming to Mary and having seen what Jesus did, believed in him. With some of them went away to the Pharisees and told them what Jesus had done. [John 11:31–46 from the Greek]

After Nicodemus read the scroll, he leaned back in his chair, contemplating what he just read. After some consideration, he said, "The chief priests have already assembled the full Sanhedrin to consider the ramifications of this one."

Nicholaus looked over at Levi, and he was already reaching for a new parchment.

Nicodemus spoke up to Levi. He said that he did not want his name on this one.

Levi nodded his understanding and began to write.

Council II

The chief priests assembled the Sanhedrin and said, "What are we going to do, for this man does many miracles? If we let him alone this way, all will believe into him, and the Romans will come and take away from us both the place and the nation.

Caiaphas, being high priest of the year, said to them, "You know nothing nor consider that it is to our benefit that one man dies for the people and not all the nation to perish." [John 11:47–50 from the Greek]

Nicholaus responded with agony in his voice, "They are going to kill him. Despite the Roman Law to the contrary, they are going to find a way to kill him."

"You are right. They are counseling together right now on how they might kill him, and they will find a way to do it. If Herod the Tetrarch can behead the Baptist, they can kill the Nazarene."

Triumphal Entry

Nicodemus came in to have his weekly visit. He was all out of breath. He sat down and paused for a moment and then was quick to share the news. "The people are looking for the Nazarene in the temple. They are asking, 'What does it seem to you that he does not at all come to the feast?' The chief priests has given a commandment that if any man knew where he is, he should inform so, that they might seize him." [John 11:56–57 from the Greek]

Nicodemus continues, "There is talk that he is in Bethany at the home of Lazarus, who had died and whom he rose from the dead [John 12:1 from the Greek]. If he is in Bethany now, he will be coming to Jerusalem. Prepare your parchments, Daniel. This is going to be an exciting time around here for the next few days."

Nicholaus could not help but think that some people are destined for certain things, and nothing will be able to keep them from it. If the Nazarene is destined to come to Jerusalem, he will, and if he does, the priests will take him, and he will die.

Nicodemus and Nicholaus just sat and looked at each other. Each of them were considering what had happened, what it all meant, and what would happen next.

*****

The market was all talk about the coming festival and whether the prophet was going to be there. The merchants were having a hard time trying to do business. Everyone was talking, and no one was buying.

Eglah and Baara were all caught up in the conversations of the day, and Levi was beginning to wish that he had found some excuse to send Daniel with them.

*****

Judas Ben-Hakkatan from Jericho came in with a scroll for Nicholaus. He came up to the table to receive his greetings.

"I have a scroll for you, my friend. I trust you still want information on the Nazarene?"

Nicholaus assured him they did and took the scroll from him. He opened it and saw that it was written in Greek, so he gave it to Daniel for translation.

"Tell me, what is the latest news from Jericho?"

"Well, I have news for you, but it's not from Jericho. As I was coming up the road, past the Mount of Olives, I saw a procession coming down from the mount and another great crowd with palm branches coming out to meet with them. The crowd had found an ass colt, and Jesus sat on it, riding into the city. Many spread their garments and branches, which they had cut from the fields, along the way. And they that followed were crying out, 'Hosanna! Blessed is he coming in the name of the Lord, the King of Israel. Blessed is the kingdom that cometh, the kingdom of our father David. Hosanna in the highest.' And he entered into Jerusalem (Mark 11:8–11 and John 12:12–14 from the Greek).

Nicholaus said, "It was a colt, the son of an ass."

Daniel, with a puzzled look on his face, asked, "How did you know that?"

"It's recorded in the Zechariah scroll. I remember it well. 'Rejoice greatly, O daughter of Zion! Shout, O daughter of Jerusalem! Behold your king comes to you! He is righteous and victorious; lowly and riding on an ass, even on a colt, the son of an ass' (Zech. 9:9 from the

Hebrew). If you would be so kind, write it all up and label it 'Ben-Hakkatan I.'"

Daniel set aside what he was doing and started writing a new scroll.

Nicholaus and Ben-Hakkatan continued their leisure time together, and after a short time, Ben-Hakkatan excused himself and left.

*****

Baara came running into Beth Eden right to Daniel's table and started telling him all about their trip to the market and everything that the people had to say. She was talking so fast that Daniel could hardly understand what she was saying.

Levi and Eglah came to Levi's table, and Levi was happy for a chance to set down. He helped himself to a mug of wine and just tried to relax for a while.

Lady jumped up when they first came in and was wagging her tail, running back and forth trying to greet everyone at once.

Nicholaus and Nicodemus just looked at each other and smiled. "The extravagant energy of youth. Chemistry at work. Too bad it's all wasted on the young," Nicholaus said.

In time, Nicodemus excused himself, and Nicholaus was left with the excitement that comes with youth.

The centurion Manlius stopped by and said that his entire cohort had been put on high alert until Passover was done so he won't be around much for a while. With that he garbed a fig and hurried out the door.

*****

The next day, Nicodemus was back again with another story of what happened in the temple that morning.

The Nazarene entered into the temple. He began to throw out those selling and buying in the temple; also, he overturned the tables of the moneychangers and the seats of those selling the doves. And he did not allow any to carry a vessel through the temple. And he taught them, "Has it not been written, 'My house shall be called a house of prayer for all nations?' But you have made it a den of robbers"(Mark 11:15–18 from the Greek).

"He did it again. He ran everybody off, and this time, he accused them of making his house a den of robbers."

"Interesting," reflected Nicholaus: "Last time, two years ago, it was a 'house of merchandise.' Now it's 'a den of robbers. Sounds like they have raised their prices too high. Is he under arrest?"

"No. The people all gathered around to hear him teach, and the priests were afraid to take him for the people all hung unto him listening (Luke 19:48 from the Greek). When he was done teaching, he left the city. Some say he went back to Bethany, but I don't know for sure."

Many of the men from the first floor became aware of the story, and they all gathered around to hear what happened. Their questions were never ending, and little, if anything else, was done that day.

Levi was busy writing. This one he labeled "Nicodemus I."

46

Zaccheus

Daniel, Eglah, and Baara were in the market, and things were somewhat back to normal after all the turmoil of yesterday. Eglah insisted that they stop at the shop of Towb Ben-Rawkal, only to find that Towb wasn't there but that his son was. She wanted to introduce Towb to Daniel, but that would have to wait. While they were there, Eglah picked out a new robe for Daniel that made him look more like a native of Jerusalem. A leisurely time of conversation ensued. After a while, everyone expressed their thanks and blessings all around, and then the girls went on with their shopping. Daniel was extra attentive to the girls. Eglah thought it was funny, and Baara was delighted with the attention.

*****

Nicodemus came in for the third day in a row. He sat down with a sad look on his face. "I'm sorry, my friend, but it is all over. The elders have decided that we are going to go from being passive observers to being active participants in the pursuit of the Nazarene. There will be no more scrolls coming in from the field. Anyone who shows up with a scroll is to be sent to the secretary's office. This is your final payment for services rendered along with many thanks from the council for a job well done." With that, Nicodemus gave Nicholaus a large pouch full of coins.

Nicholaus was disappointed, but he knew that it wouldn't last. "I have one more scroll for you. It came up from Jericho. He rummaged around his table and handed Nicodemus a scroll marked "Ben-Hakkatan I."

Nicodemus unrolled the scroll and began to read.

Hakkatan I

I, Judas Ben Hakkatan from Jericho, bring you greetings from the High Holy One of Israel.

Jesus was passing through Jericho. And a man named Zaccheus, who was the chief tax collector and he was rich, was seeking to see Jesus, as to who he is. He was not able because of the crowd as he was little in stature. And running ahead, he went up onto a sycamore tree, so that he might see him; for he was going to pass that way.

As he came to the place, looking up, Jesus saw him, and said to him, Zaccheus, hurry, come down, for today I must stay in your house. And hastening he came down and welcomed him rejoicing. [Luke 19:1–10 from the Greek]

The Lord bless you and keep you. The Lord make His face to shine upon you and be gracious to you. The Lord lift up his countenance upon you and give you peace. [Num. 6:24–26 from the Hebrew]

"Interesting. I know Zaccheus. He was notorious for his shady dealings. This may be an interesting time to live in Jericho. But I can't take this back with me, so you can just add it to your collection if you want to. Also, you need to know that Ben-Paulus has been assigned to lead a detail to report on and possibly cause the apprehension of the Nazarene. He will be giving written reports to the secretary. I have made arrangements with one of the undersecretaries, who is a follower, to make a copy of his report for me. I will be passing them on to you for your collections. I think the day is coming when someone outside our circle has preserved the factual history."

After their normal time of relaxation and refreshment, Nicodemus left.

*****

Later that afternoon, Towb Ben-Rawkal came in all smiles and happy to greet his old friend Nicholaus.

Lady came around the table to give him her welcome dance. "My goal in life is to become as wonderful as this dog thinks I am." He picked Lady up and held her in his lap. She put her paws on his shoulders and began to give him doggy kisses. He laughed with delight and then put her back on the floor.

"Consider yourself one of the very few. That dog is a good judge of character, and not many receive that kind of a greeting."

Both men enjoyed the moment, and then Ben-Rawkal said that he had just come up from Jericho. "I saw your Nazarene coming up out of the city, and I thought you might like to know what I saw for your project."

My project is becoming the worst-kept secret in Jerusalem, Nicholaus thought to himself as he gave that look to Levi.

Levi began writing.

Ben-Rawkal I

"The blind son of Timeus Bar-Timeus was sitting beside the highway, begging. Hearing that it was Jesus the Nazarene he began to cry out saying: "Son of David, Jesus, have mercy on me!"

Many warned him that he be quiet. But he much more cried out: "Son of David, Jesus, have mercy on me!"

Then standing still, Jesus said for him to be called.

They called the blind one, saying to him: "Be comforted, rise up, he calls you."

Rising up he came to Jesus.

Jesus said to him, "What do you desire I should do to you?"

The blind one said to him, "My Lord, that I may see again."

Jesus said to him, "Go, your faith has healed you."

And instantly, he saw again and followed Jesus up the highway. [Mark 10:46–52 from the Greek]

"Again it is 'Go, your faith has healed you.' More and more, Levi's evaluation of the spirit world is proving true. Calling on Jesus in faith will make it come true."

Levi finished the scroll and gave it to Nicholaus.

Ben-Rawkal enjoyed a leisure time with his friend Nicholaus and in time wished blessings on all and departed.

Mary's Anointing

I t was a normal day at the market. There was an aroma of fresh food in the air and the merchants were barking out their wares. Daniel was relegated to escort duty again. It seems that this has become one of his regular duties now. The talk in the market was centered around Jesus being at the home of his friend, Lazarus, in Bethany, and that there was going to be a supper in his honor that night. It sounded like everyone was going to go and see what would happen. Eglah decided that she just had to convince Levi to go.

*****

Nicodemus had a new report for Nicholaus when he came in that morning. "I just came from the temple and the chief priest and the elders came near to him and asked, 'By what authority do you do these things? And who gave you this authority?'

"And answering Jesus said to them, 'I also will ask you one thing, which if you tell me, I also will tell you by what authority I do things. John's baptism, from where was it from? From heaven or from man?'

"After a pause and conversation among themselves, they said, 'We do not know.'

"Jesus replied, 'Neither do I tell you by what authority I do these things.'"

Nicodemus went on with his report. "If they had said that it was from heaven, Jesus would have asked them, 'Why did you not believe him?' If they had said that it was from man, they fear the people. For all hold John to be a prophet (Matt 21:23–27 from the Greek).

Levi recorded it all as "Nicodemus II."

Nicholaus reflected that they still regard him as an imposter, possessed with the power of Beelzebub, delegating to himself an authority that he did not have. Self-proclaimed prophets were a part of history, and to them, he was but one more charlatan that needed to be done away with. "Do not envy evil men nor desire to be with them. For their hearts study violence and their lips talk of mischief" (Prov. 24:1–2 from the Hebrew).

"Yes, but you must admit to the cleverness of the man. He seems able to deal with whatever confronts him and by whoever the presenter is." Levi reflected almost as to himself. "Answer not a fool according to his foolishness, lest you become like him" (Prov. 26:4 from the Hebrew).

The conversation continued into the late hours of the afternoon when finally the subject was talked out, and the men retired to their separate ways.

*****

Early the next day, Levi came in, went right to his table, ignoring everything, and began to write.

Levi III

On the sixth day before Passover, Jesus came to Bethany, where Lazarus was, who had died. It was he whom Jesus raised from the dead.

They made him a supper, and Martha served. Lazarus was one of those reclining with him.

A great crowd of people learned that he was there, and they did not come because of Jesus alone, but that they also might see Lazarus whom he raised from the dead.

Taking a pound of the ointment spikenard*, Mary anointed the feet of Jesus and wiped of his feet with her hair. The house was filled with the odor of the ointment.

Judas Iscariot*, one of his disciples said, "Why was this ointment not sold for three hundred denarii and given to the poor?"

Then Jesus said, "Allow her, for she has kept it for the day of my burial. You always have the poor with you, but you do not always me. [John 12:1–11 from the Greek]

This is the second time Jesus was anointed. (See the "Galileans XI and XII scrolls.)

Levi finished his writing and gave the scroll to Nicholaus.

Nicholaus unrolled and read the scroll. "Allow her, for she has kept it for the day of my burial.' He is already anticipating his death. He must know what is in store for him."

"I agree with your evaluation of her act, but look at the love. Judas points out the extravagance of the act. Does not the value of the gift express her love? And see her humility. To step out and wash his feet in this manner. She uncovered her head and wiped his feet with her hair. I marveled at what I witnessed."

"Truly he is a most remarkable man." With that, both men went to work.

*****

That midday, Nicholaus went upstairs for his weekly meal with Mistress Abishag. They had their usual small talk, and Nicholaus said that Manlius told him that they were getting ready to clean out all the malefactors from the Antonia dungeon and crucify them.

"You know, of course, that one of them is one of mine."

"Really? Tell me more."

"The one they call Bar-Abbas was born right upstairs. He was the bastard son of one of my girls. She didn't know who the father was for sure, so she named him Polus Abbas ("many fathers"). He picked up the *Bar* up in Galilee when he joined the Zealots. He lived here on the third floor until he reached that age, and then I had to kick him out."

"Interesting. Tell me, is he the only one?"

'Oh, no. There have been others, and some of them turned out to be first-class citizens. But this one was nothing but trouble from day one. I was happy to see him go."

The conversation turned to the lighter side of current affairs, and a pleasant time was had by both of them.

48

Anointed by a Woman

On the day before Passover, Levi came in and went right to Nicholaus. "I need to see you in the security rooms. I have something to ask you about that must be private."

The men retired to the security rooms. Nicholaus could not imagine what could be so secret.

After they entered the rooms and the door was closed, Levi explained, "That woman is going to be the death of me yet. At times, I just don't understand her."

"Now, now, settle down and tell me what happened."

"Eglah and I went to the home of Simon the Leper in Bethany to witness the supper that has been prepared for Jesus the Nazarene. While we were there, Eglah stepped out and anointed Jesus, just like Mary, the sister of Lazarus, did four day ago. Now I fear for her safety. If the authorities identify her, there is no telling what they will do."

Nicholaus was dumbfounded at what he had just been told. He paused in deep thought and then said, "First of all, and this is very important, we need a record of that event. You are going to have to write it up. Secondly, Eglah has got to stay out of public places, where she could be identified. No more trips to the market or even here." Nicholaus was in deep thought again for a moment, and then he said, "Go ahead and write it up, but only say it was a woman, and nothing else that might link the anointing to Eglah. I am going up to the third floor and have a talk with Mistress Abishag. I want to see if she can send Baara to the market with Daniel for the next few days instead of sending Eglah. Eglah must stay at home for a while. As fast as things are happening right now, it should be safe for her to go out again in a few days, after the Passover."

Levi was in agreement with that plan, but he was not too sure about keeping Eglah at home. "That girl has developed a mind of her own." He thought as he returned to his table. He took up a new parchment and began to write. Nicholaus headed to the third floor, with staff in hand.

Levi IV

I was witness to a supper prepared by Simon the Leper, at his home in Bethany. Jesus the Nazarene and the twelve were the honored guest.

Jesus was reclining at the supper, and a woman came out with her Alabaster Vial of pure costly ointment of Nard, and breaking the Alabaster Vial she poured it down his head.

Some were indignant towards her, saying among themselves: "For what has this waste of ointment occurred? For this could be sold for over three hundred denarii, and given to the poor." And they were incensed with her

Jesus said: "Let her alone. Why do you cause her troubles? She worked a good work toward me. For you have the poor with you always, and when you wish you can do well toward them. But you do not have me always. What this one held, she did. She took beforehand to anoint my body for the burial. Truly I say to you, wherever this gospel is proclaimed in all the world, what this one did will also be spoken of for a memorial of her. [Mark 14:3–9 from the Greek]

Levi read the scroll more than twice before he gave it to Nicholaus who had just returned from the third floor. "I had a talk with Mistress Abishag, and she is in agreement with the plan. Eglah can take as much time as she wants. Most of all, she wants her to be safe."

Nicholaus quickly read the scroll and dropped it to his lap. "This will do. You have covered the basics, and that is all we need. I still can't believe that she really did that."

Levi nodded his head yes.

Nicholaus just shook his head and said, "That girl will never cease to amaze me."

*****

Nicodemus came in with a new scroll. He seated himself and handed the scroll to Nicholaus. "I think you are going to like this one." He then helped himself to some bread and wine.

Nicholaus smiled at his friend and unrolled it and began to read.

Paulus III

I was assigned a group of young men to help me observe. We witnessed the Sadducees, who say there is no resurrection, come to Jesus and question him saying: "Teacher, Moses said: 'If anyone should die not having children, his brother shall marry his wife and shall raise up seed to his brother.' There were seven brothers with us. The first was married, but he expired without having a child with his wife. He left his wife to his brother. In the same way also, the second and the third to the seventh. Last of all, the woman also died. Then in the resurrection, of which of the seven will she be the wife of? For all had her."

Jesus said to them, "You are not knowing the Scriptures nor the power of God. For in the resurrection, they neither marry nor are given in marriage, but they are as angels of God in heaven. But concerning the resurrection of the dead, have you not read that which was spoken to you by God? 'I am the God of Abraham and the God of Isaac and the God of Jacob?' God is not God of the dead but of the living."

Hearing this, the crowds were astonished at his teaching. [Matt. 22:23–32 from the Greek]

Hearing that he had silenced the Sadducees, we were gathered together. One of us, a lawyer questioned him to test him: "Teacher, which is the great commandment in the law?"

Jesus said to him, "'You shall love the Lord your God with all your heart and with all your soul and with all your mind.' This is the first and great commandment. And the second is like it. 'You shall love your neighbor as your-self.' On these two commandments all the Law and Prophets hang." [Matt. 22:34–40 from the Greek]

I have nothing else to record at this time.

Nicholaus reflected on the contents of the scroll and then said, "The Sadducees do not believe in the resurrection of the dead, so they must have been trying to show what they believe to be the absurdity of the doctrine. Jesus in turn challenged their knowledge of the scriptures, and it seems that they did not have an answer for him."

This time, it was the Sadducees followed by the Pharisees. Before that, it was the Pharisees and the Herodians teaming up on him," Levi exclaimed. "What's next, the Essenes?"

Nicholaus smiled and said, "I don't think so, you will never see an Essene in the temple as long as they think temple worship has been corrupted."

The men continued with their morning reprieve, and Levi went back to work.

Was It Legal?

Baara was excited; this was her first trip to the market without Eglah's supervision. Besides, she would have some time alone with Daniel. She held tight to his arm as they went from stall to stall. Baara had her signature silk head dress on to identify her as Eglah's servant, and she was surprised to find that the merchants were giving her the same respect that they gave to Eglah.

The market was crowded with the new people that had come to the city for Passover. The silent talk among the followers of Jesus was the crucifixions and the release of Bar-Abbas instead of the Master. Many of the people she expected to see were absent, and she was afraid that they were in hiding as Eglah was. Still, it was a bright shiny day, and she was out with Daniel—what could be better?

Beth Eden was abuzz with activity, but little work was done. Everybody was talking about the events of the day, the new people on the second floor, the crucifixions at the Damascus Gate, and for some, and the fate of Jesus the Nazarene. Strange events make for strange bedfellows.

The gathering around Nicholaus's table was an odd one. First, there was the Roman centurion Manlius; and then there was Malchus, the slave of Caiaphas; Ahikar Bar-Jathan, from Cana; and Nicodemus. Levi and Daniel pulled their tables and chairs over so everyone could be comfortable. Daniel recorded it all and called it "Daniel I."

Malchus was at Caiaphas's house and he was explaining how Jesus was taken into custody early Friday morning.

Ahikar Bar-Jathan explained how Jesus had been betrayed by Judas Iscariot. He said that he had sought out his friend, Nathanael Bar-Tholomew, in Bethany and that this is what Nathanael had told him.

Nicholaus then asked, "Who authorized his arrest, and who were the witnesses that brought charges against him?"

Malchus responded, "Caiaphas authorized the arrest, and there were no witnesses to bring charges against him."

Looking at Nicodemus, Nicholaus asked, "Isn't that against the law? There can be no arrests until two or more witnesses bringing charges to the court."

Nicodemus nodded his agreement.

Malchus then said, "Oh, it gets better, now hear the rest. Jesus was taken before Annas and was examined by him. Then he was taken before Caiaphas for further examination" (John 18:2–23 from the Greek).

Nicholaus then asked, "Annas is no longer an active priest. Does he have the authority to question anyone?"

Nicodemus agreed that he had none.

Nicholaus continues, "And was it not Caiaphas, speaking about Jesus, who said that it was advantageous for one man to perish for the people? If so, he, and everyone who agreed with him, had a pre-disposed prejudice that made them ineligible to act as judges. They all must excuse themselves. Also, all of this was done before the first morning sacrifice, which also makes the whole action illegal."

Nicodemus then added to the report. "In the morning, before the first sacrifice, some of the Sanhedrin were called together. Many witnesses were brought in to testify falsely against him, but their statements did not agree. They said that they heard him say that he would destroy the temple and in three days rebuild it. Yet even then, their testimonies did not agree.

"Caiaphas then stood up and asked: "Are you not going to answer? What is this testimony that these men are bringing against you?" Jesus remained silent and gave no answer.

Caiaphas then asked him: "Are you the Christ, the son God?" Jesus answered: "I am, and you will see the Son of Man sitting at the right hand of God, and coming on the clouds of heaven."

Caiaphas then tore his robe and stated: "why do we need any more witnesses. You have heard the blasphemy. What do you think?"

Nicodemus continued his report by saying: "Jesus was then condemned as worthy of death. Later, after the first sacrifice the whole Sanhedrin was called together to confirm what had been done earlier." (Matt. 26:59–66 from the Greek). I am convinced that this entire procedure was totally illegal."

Manlius said, "I was in the palace when Jesus was brought before the governor. The governor asked him, 'Are the king of the Jews?' Jesus replied, 'You say it.' He was then accused of many things by the priests and the elders, but he answered nothing. Pilatus said to him, 'Do you not hear how many things they are testifying against you?' And he did not answer him, not even one word.

"Pilate then offered the crowd to release a prisoner to them. They could have Jesus or Bar-Abbas. They chose Bar-Abbas. Pilate then asked, 'What then should I do to Jesus?' And they said, 'Let him be crucified!' Pilate then washed his hands before the crowd, saying, 'I am innocent of the blood of this just one.' They answered, 'Let his blood be on us and on our children.' With that, Pilate released Bar-Abbas to them. And after flogging Jesus, he delivered him up that he might be crucified" (Matt. 27:11–26 from the Greek).

Nicodemus then asked, "How much punishment can one man take? I have been in the home of Caiaphas, and he has a dry cistern in his lower level, for holding prisoners, and it is very cold. There is also a flogging station right at the bottom of the stairs on the right."

Malchus then said that Jesus was held in that cistern when he was not being questioned.

Manlius then added, "And he was not flogged by Jewish law, but by my soldiers. The man was almost dead when it was over. Then we crucified him outside the gate at the place of the skull, between

Bar-Achan and Bar-Dimeus, the Zealots who were taken with Bar-Abbas. I could not help but marvel at the man. Truly he was the Son of God."

Ahikar Bar-Jathan explained that his friend Nathanael Bar-Tholomew said something else that the Nazarene told them the night he was taken. He said, "Do not let your heart be troubled. You believe in God. Believe also in me. In my Father's house are many dwelling places. If it were not so, I would have told you. I am going to prepare a place for you! And if I go and prepare a place for you, I am coming again and will receive you to myself that where I am you may be also" (John 14:2–3 from the Greek).

Nicodemus said, "That is what a bridegroom would tell his bride."

At this point, Levi stood up and boldly declared, "Jesus is going to be risen from the dead, just like Lazarus was!"

Rise Again

Levi was on his feet, and his excitement was clear to everyone.

Daniel started a new scroll, "Daniel II."

Looking at Nicodemus, Levi said, "Remember what Jesus said when we were in the garden: 'That which receiving birth from the flesh is flesh and that receiving birth from the spirit is spirit.' We have been looking at this through eyes of flesh when we should have been looking at this through eyes of the spirit."

"Remember what he said when he was asked to give a sign about the sign of Jonah? Let me go get the scroll."

Levi hurried to the security rooms and returned with a scroll. He unrolled it and began to read.

> Jonah was swallowed up by a great fish for three days and three nights. The first thing he did was to pray to the Lord his God out of the belly of the fish and said,
>
> > I cried out to Jehovah, from my distresses. And he answered me. Out of the belly of Sheol, I cried for help, and you heard my voice. For you cast me into the deep, into the heart of the seas, and the current surrounded me. All your breakers and your waves passed over me.

I said I am cast off from Your eyes, yet I will again look to your holy temple. Waters encompassed me even to my soul. The depth closed around me; seaweed was clinging to my head. I went down to the bases of the mountains; the earth with her bars was about me forever.

But you brought up my life from the pit, O Jehovah, my God. When my soul fainted within me, I remembered Jehovah; and my prayer came to you, to your Holy temple. Those who observe vanities of idolatry forsake their faithfulness, but I will sacrifice to you with the voice of thanksgiving; I will fulfill that which I have vowed. Salvation belongs to Jehovah.

And Jehovah spoke to the fish, and it vomited Jonah out onto the dry land. [Jonah 2:1-11 from the Hebrew]

Levi continued, "Jesus said he would spend three days and three nights in the center of the earth. Eyes of the flesh would see this as a grave, but the eyes of the spirit would see this as the heart of the world. What is the heart of the world? What is the one thing you will find anywhere you go? Is it not sin?

"Jesus died upon the cross. Manlius was there and witnessed it. Jonas did not die in the belly of the fish. Therefore the interpretation is not of the flesh but of the spirit. We have to look at it through eyes of the spirit.

"Jehovah has heaped all the sins of the world on Jesus, just as he heaped all the billows and the waves of the sea upon Jonas. His crucifixion has the sacrifice of the Lamb of God. It became the sacrifice for the sins of the world as represented by the billows and the waves of the sea upon Jonas. If Jehovah accepts that sacrifice, Jesus will rise from the dead just like Lazarus did."

"Also I believe that King David was allowed to see this salvation, and he recorded what he saw in the psalms. David wasn't writing about any king, but *the* King. He wasn't writing about himself but the King of kings!"

Levi then took up a scroll he had been studying. He found the section he was looking for and began to read the Hebrew and then speaking in Greek.

> To the chief musician. A Psalm of David.
>
> The king rejoices in your strength, O Jehovah; and how greatly does he rejoice in your salvation. You have given him his heart's desire and have not withheld the prayer of his lips.
>
> Selah.
>
> For you will precede him with blessings of goodness; you set a crown of pure gold on his head. He asked life from you: you gave to him length of days forever and ever. His glory is great in Your salvation; You have laid honor and majesty on him.
>
> For you have set him blessings for ever; you have rejoiced him in the Joy of your face. For the King trust in Jehovah, and in the mercy of the Most High; he shall not be moved.
>
> Your hand shall find out all your enemies; your right hand shall find out those who hate you. You shall set them as a fiery furnace in the time of your presence; Jehovah will swallow them up in his wrath, and the firer shall devour them. You shall destroy their fruit from the earth, and their seed from among the sons of men. For they stretched forth evil against You; they imagined a plot; they cannot prevail, for you shall make them turn the back; You shall make ready Your arrows on Your strings against their faces.
>
> Be exalted, O Jehovah, in Your strength; so, we will sing, and sing Psalms of Your power."
> [Psalm 21 from the Hebrew]

To the chief musician; on the deer of the down. A Psalm of David.

My God, my God, why have you forsaken me, and are far from my deliverance, and from the words of my groaning? O my God, I try by day but you do not answer; and in the night, but there is no silence to me. But you are Holy, being in throne on Israel's praises. Our fathers trusted in you; they trusted, and you delivered them. They cried to you and were delivered; they trusted in you, and were not ashamed.

But I am a worm, and no man; a reproach of mankind, and despised by the people. All who see me scornfully laugh at me; they open the lip; they shake their head, saying, he rolled on Jehovah, let Him deliver him; let Him rescue him, since He delights in him.

For You are he who took me out of the womb, causing me to trust on my mother's breast. I was cast on you from the womb; from my mother's belly, you are my God. Be not far from me; for trouble is near; because no one is here to help. Many bulls have circled around me; strong bulls of Bashan have surrounded me. They open their mouth on me, like a lion ripping and roaring. I am poured out like waters, and all my bones are spread apart; my heart is like wax; it is melded in the midst of my bowels., is dried up like a potsherd; and my tall claims to my jaws; also you appointed me to the dust of death; for dogs had encircled me; a band of spoilers and hemmed me and, pierces of my hands and my feet. I count all my bones.

They look, they stare at me, they divide my garments among them, they make fall a lot for my clothing. But you, O Jehovah, be not far off; hurry to help me! Deliver my soul from the sword, my only one from the paw of the dog, save me from the lion's mouth; and from the horns of the wild oxen. You have answered me.

I will declare Your name to my brothers; I will praise you in the midst of the assembly. Youth who fear Jehovah, praise him; all the seed of Jacob glorify him; and all the seed of Israel, near him. For he has not despised nor hated the affliction of the afflicted and he has not hidden his space from him, but when he tried to him. He heard.

My praise shall be of you in the great assembly; I will pay my vows before the ones who fear him. The meek shall eat and be satisfied; those who seek Jehovah shall praise Him; your heart shall live forever. All the ends of the earth shall remember and turn to Jehovah; and all the families of the nations shall worship before you.

For the kingdom is Jehovah; and he is the ruler amongst the nations. All the fat ones of the earth have eaten, and have worshiped; all those going down to the dust shall bow before Him; and he kept not his own soul alive. A seed shall serve him; it shall be spoken of the Lord to the coming generation; they shall come and shall declare his righteousness to the people that shall yet be born; he has done it." [Psalm 22 from the Hebrew]

A Psalm of David.

Jehovah is my shepherd; I shall not want. He makes me lie down in green pastures; He leads me to restful waters; He restores my soul; He guides me in the paths of righteousness for His name sake. Yea, though I walk through the valley of the shadow of death, I will fear no evil;

for you are with me; your rod and your staff, they comfort me.

You prepare a table before me before my enemies; You anoint my head with oil; my cup runs over. Surely goodness and mercy shall follow me all the days of my life; and I shall dwell in the house of Jehovah, for as long as my days. [Psalm 23 from the Hebrew]

Levi laid the scroll aside. He smiled as he had never smiled before and said, "Behold our salvation. Jesus will rise from the dead on the third day, just as Jonah came forth from the big fish and Lazarus from the tomb. He will ascend into heaven and be with his Father forever. It's all right here in the scriptures. All we ever had to do was read it with spiritual eyes to really understand it."

The men all sat in silence and wonder at what they had just heard.

51

Into Thy Hands

The women of the commons were gathered on the grounds as was their daily morning custom. All the talk was about the men being at the trial of the Nazarene and how he was to be crucified.

Eglah could not contain herself. She had her friend, Zibiah, take care of Huldah, and she headed for the Damascus Gate.

Going through the gate, she saw the chief priests gathered together, just a short way down the road on her right. And there was Jesus on a cross, crucified like a common criminal. *How could they? What had he done? This all had to be a terrible mistake,* she thought.

Eglah saw some of the women she knew to be followers, and she moved up behind them to watch

Eglah heard Jesus say, "Father, forgive them, for they do not know what they are doing" (Luke 23:34 from the Greek).

And on the sixth hour, darkness came over all the land until the ninth hour. And at the ninth hour, Jesus cried with a loud voice, "My God, my God, why did you forsake me?" (Mark 15:33–34 from the Greek). Then crying with a loud voice, Jesus said, "Father, into your hands I commit my spirit." And after saying this, he breathed out his spirit (Luke 23:44–46 from the Greek).

Eglah went with the other women as they followed the men who carried the body of Jesus and beheld the tomb. They all returned to the city and prepared spices and ointments for his anointing.

*****

Meanwhile, Levi returned home to find the house empty. He hurried about finding his family and eventually went to the home of Eglah's friend Zibiah. He found Huldah there along with an explanation of the day's events.

Levi didn't know if he should be mad at his wife or proud of her. He finally decided to be a little of both.

Eglah was just coming down the road as Levi and Huldah were arriving back home. She ran to them crying and hugged her family. "They crucified him," she whimpered through her tears. "They crucified him and stuck him in a stone cold tomb for the Sabbath, and they didn't even properly prepare his body for burial."

Levi tried to soothe his wife but found that it was like dipping into the pool of Salome without getting wet.

Eglah then proclaimed that the women were going to go to the tomb after Sabbath and properly prepare his body.

Levi resolved himself to the fact that Eglah was going to do what Eglah was going to do. And the best thing for him to do was stay out of the way and take care of Hulda.

*****

The high priest anticipated that there was going to be a backlash to their demand that the Nazarene be crucified, but it was much larger than they estimated.

The events in the Court of the Gentiles had dug deep into their expected revenues. And now there was a large reduction in the number of sacrifices being made. At least, with the Nazarene gone, there was a chance that things would return to normal next year.

The veil had been rent in two, so that was going to have to be repaired. And the earthquakes had done some damage that was going to have to be taken care of. The herdsman and the moneychangers were all demanding relief from their losses, but they were just going to have to get along with what was left, the same way the temple was.

*****

The next day, the chief priests and the Pharisees were gathered to Pilatus. They were saying, "Sir, we have recalled that the deceiver said while living, 'After three days, I will rise.' Therefore command that the grave be secured until the third day that his disciples may not come by night and steal him away and may say to the people, 'He has risen from the dead.' And the last deception will be worse than the first."

Pilatus said to them, "You have a guard. Go away and make it as secure as you know how."

So they made the grave secure, sealing the stone along with a guard (Matt. 27:63–66 from the Greek).

*****

Nicholaus went to the temple on the Sabbath. It was his duty, but actually, it was more out of habit. When he returned home, he went straight to his study. He had to open the scriptures and read again that which Levi had read the day before. Was it possible that the truth had been right there before their eyes all these years and no one saw it until now? Three days and three nights? The seas; and the current surrounded me? Waters encompassed me even to my soul. The depth closed around me; seaweed was clinging to my head. I went down to the bases of the mountains; the Earth with her bars was about me forever.? I will sacrifice to you with the voice of thanksgiving; I will fulfill that which I have vowed. Salvation belongs to Jehovah? "My God, my God, why have you forsaken me", and are far from my deliverance, and from the words of my groaning? Many bulls have circled around me; strong bulls of Bashan have surrounded me. They open their mouth on me, like a lion ripping and roaring? You have answered me. I will declare Your name to my brothers; I will praise you in the midst of the assembly? A seed shall serve him; it shall be spoken of the Lord to the coming generation; they shall come and shall declare his righteousness to the people that shall yet be born; he has done it?

Could it be? Is this Jesus the sacrificial Lamb of God? Has he answered for all the sins of the world for all time? That is what the psalmist is saying. Could it really be?

52

It Was Empty

Malchus, the servant of Caiaphas, paid a surprise visit to Nicholaus.

"With all that is going on right now, I never expected to see you," Nicholaus said as he rose to greet his friend. "I expected you to be very busy."

"I made some excuses to come and have contracts written so I could see you and bring you up-to-date. My master was concerned about the preparation for Passover, and he didn't want the bodies to remain on the crosses until the Sabbath. He asked Pilate that their legs be broken and they be taken away. I don't know if this should be part of your project, but I thought you would like to know it" (John 19:32 from the Greek).

Nicholaus thanked his friend for the information and settled in to a brief time of relaxation and small talk.

*****

Hakkatan, a servant of the council secretary Ben-Hilkiah, came in later and stated that even though the scroll program had ended, the secretary wanted to maintain contact. "Nicodemus is not available for some unknown reason. So the secretary sent me... Actually, I know where Nicodemus is. He is with Joseph of Arimathea, who went to Pilatus and begged for the body of Jesus. Pilate called the centurion and asked him if he died long ago. And knowing from the centurion, he granted the body to Joseph.

"They brought a linen cloth and took him down. They wrapped him in linen and laid him in a tomb, which was cut out of rock, and they rolled a stone to the mouth of the tomb" (Mark 15:43–46 from the Greek).

Nicholaus thanked his friend and asked him to stay a while and refresh himself.

Hakkatan said, "Thank you, but I really can't. I have got to get back to the council's office. There is much to do during these hectic times." With that, he departed.

Nicholaus then busied himself writing up the information he had just received. He labeled it "Nicholaus I."

*****

It was time for the midday meal before Eglah got home. Levi had been concerned, but he didn't scold her. He knew that wherever she had been was important. She would never leave the baby alone that long if it wasn't.

Eglah was all excited to tell Levi the news. She, Mary Magdalene, Joanna, Mary the mother of James, and the other women who followed Jesus had gone to the tomb to bring the spices they had prepared so that they might anoint him. "Very early, we came upon the tomb. And one of us asked, 'Who will roll away the stone from the mouth of the tomb for us?' But when we looked up, we saw that the stone had been rolled back for it was very large. And when we entered into the tomb, we saw a young man sitting on the right clothed in a white robe. And we were much amazed.

"But he said to us, 'Do not be amazed. You seek Jesus the Nazarene, who has been crucified. He has risen. He is not here. See the place where they put him? But go, say to the disciples and to Peter, "He goes before you into Galilee. You will see him there, even as he told you."' We went out quickly and fled from the tomb. Trembling and ecstasy took hold of us, and we told no one, not a thing, we were afraid" (Mark 16:2–8 from the Greek).

"We rushed back from the tomb and reported all things to the eleven and to all the rest. And our words seemed like foolishness to them, and they did not believe them" (Luke 24: 9–11 from the Greek).

Levi then exclaimed, "He has risen, just like it was proclaimed in the Psalms of David! He has risen, and there is a whole new world for us to enter into! This is the most wonderful of news that you could bring me." He then busied himself writing down everything that Eglah had told him. He labeled it "Eglah II."

*****

Two days later, Simon Ben-Cleopas came in, and Levi reached for a new parchment the instant he saw him.

He went straight to Nicholaus and sat down, all excited to tell his story:

> My friend and I were on our way home from Jerusalem, and we were talking about all these things taking place. And it happened as we talked and reasoned that a man came near and traveled with us, and he said to us, "What words are these which you exchange with each other while walking, and why do you look distressed?"
>
> I answered him, "Are you only a stranger in Jerusalem and do not know the things happening in it these days?"
>
> "What things?"
>
> "The things concerning Jesus the Nazarene, who was a man, a prophet mighty in deed and word before God and all the people. And how the chief priests and our rulers delivered him to the judgment of death and crucified him. But we were hoping that he is the one going to redeem

Israel. But then with all these things, this brings today the third day since these things happen. And also some of our women astounded us, who reported having been early at the tomb and not finding his body. They came saying they have seen a vision of angels, who said that Jesus is alive. And some of those with us went to the tomb and found it like the women said it to be so, but they did not see Jesus.

Then the stranger said to us, "Oh, fools and slow of heart to believe on all things which the prophets spoke. Was it not necessary for Christ to suffer these things and to enter into his glory?" And beginning from Moses and from all prophets, he explained to us all the scriptures."

We drew near to our home where we were going, and he seemed to be going further and we held him back, saying, "Stay with us, for it is toward evening and the day has declined." And he came to stay with us. And it happened that as he reclined with us, he took the loaf and blessed it and broke it and gave it to us. And our eyes were opened, and we knew that it was Jesus. And then he became invisible to us."

We said to each other, "Were not our hearts burning in us as he spoke to us on the road and as he opened up to us the scriptures?"

And rising up in the same hour, we came back to Jerusalem, and we found the eleven and those with them assembled. We said to them, "The Lord really was raised and appeared to us." And we related the things on the highway and how he was known to us in the breaking of the loaf.

As we were telling these things, Jesus himself stood in our midst and said to us, "Peace to you!" We were terrified and filled with fear. We thought we saw a spirit.

And he said to us, "Why are you troubled? And why do reasons come up in your heart? See my hands and my feet so you will believe that I am he. Feel me and see because a spirit does not have flesh and bones as you see me having." At that, he showed us his hands and feet. Yet we did not believe for the joy and the marveling. He said to us, "Have you any food here?" And someone handed a broiled part of a fish to him. He took it and ate before us. (Luke 24:13–43 from the Greek)

Nicholaus smiled a smile of understanding and then invited him to relax and have something to eat.

Levi finished the scroll and labeled it "Ben-Cleopas I."

Eglah and I

Two days went by before anyone had another report. Malchus, servant of Caiaphas, came in with some remarkable stories.

Daniel took up a parchment and recorded what he had to say.

Malchus was all excited and was more than ready to tell his story.

> I was assigned accompany a crowd with swords and clubs. The order I received from the chief priests and the scribes and the elders was to go to Mount Olives and arrest Jesus the Nazarene.
>
> One of the twelve who betrayed him was with us. And he said, "Whomever I kiss, it is he. Seize him and lead him away safely." He approached him and said, "Rabbi, Rabbi." And he kissed him. We laid our hands on him at once and seized him. But one of his disciples who drew a sword struck me and took off my ear."
>
> Jesus said to us, "Have you come out with swords and clubs to take me like I'm a robber? I was with you daily teaching in the temple, and you saw me. But it is happening that the scrip-

tures may be fulfilled." And leaving him, they all fled. [Mark 14:43–50 from the Greek].

And that's not all. After the crucifixion, some of the guards came into the city and reported to the chief priests that the body of Jesus was missing. The elders and council gave enough to the soldiers, saying, 'Say that his disciples came and stole him by night, and we were asleep. And if the governor hears about this, we will persuade him and will make you free from anxiety." And taking the silver, they did as they were taught. [Matt. 28:11–15 from the Greek]

When Malchus finished his stories, he excused himself and hurried out the door.

Daniel finished the scroll and labeled it "Malchus I." He then gave it to Nicholaus for his approval.

*****

It had been about four weeks since Nicholaus had heard from Levi. He, his wife, and their baby were up in Galilee chasing the Nazarene.

Ahikar Bar-Jathan, from Cana of Galilee, came in to renew an old friendship. "Nathaniel brought me a scroll to bring down to you. Here it is."

Nicholaus thanked him. "Sit down and have something to eat while I read the scroll." He took the scroll and noticed that it was labeled "Levi III."

Greetings, in the name of the High Holy One of Israel. May you prosper in all that is important to you. May the Lord bless you and keep you. May the Lord make his face to shine upon you and be gracious to you. May the Lord lift up his countenance upon you and give you peace. [Num. 6:24–26 from the Hebrew]

Eglah and I, with our baby bound to her chest, went with the others and the eleven disciples into Galilee to the appointed mount where Jesus was to meet them. We saw him and worshiped him. But we doubted.

Jesus said, "All authority in heaven and on earth was given to me. Therefore go, disciple all nations, baptizing them in the name of the Father and of the Son and of the Holy Spirit, teaching them to observe whatever I commanded you. And behold, I am with you until the completion of the age." [Matt. 28:16–20 from the Greek]

We then followed them to Bethany. There he charged us not to leave Jerusalem but to await the promise of the Father: "For John indeed baptized in water, but you will be baptized in the Holy Spirit that many days after these" [Acts 1:5, from the Greek].

We questioned him, saying, "Lord, do you restore the kingdom to Israel at this time?"

He said to us, "It is not yours to know times or seasons, which the Father placed in his own authority, but you will receive power, the Holy Spirit, coming upon you, and you will be witnesses for me both in Jerusalem and in all Judea and Samaria and in all of the earth."

As we looked on, he was taken up and a cloud received him.

As we were looking intently into the heaven, two men in white clothing stood by us and said, "Men, Galileans, why do you stand looking up to the heaven? This Jesus, the one being taken from you into heaven, will come in the way you saw him going into heaven."

We returned to Jerusalem, and we went in the way to the upper room where they were waiting; both Peter and James and John, and Andrew, Philip and Thomas, Bartholomew, Matthew and James the son of LPS and Simon and Judah's, the brother of James. [Acts 1:13 from the Greek].

As we went, Eglah had her head on my shoulder, crying. I said to her, "Do not cry. This is not the end, this is just the beginning."

THE SCROLL OF TERMS

Alabaster:
A hard translucent variety of gypsum, unsurely white and sometimes banded.

Antonia:
The Antonia Fortress, on the northwest corner of the temple.

Bangle:
A bracelet.

Bar:
(Aramaic) The son of. Followed by his father's name, the name
of some prominent family member, or the name of someone he is a
follower of.

Bat:
(Hebrew) The daughter of. Followed by her mother's name, the
name of some prominent family member, or the name of someone
she is a follower of.

Beelzebub's scribe:
The devil's advocate.

Ben:
(Hebrew) The son of. Followed by his father's name, the name
of some prominent family member, or the name of someone he is a
follower of.

Berossus:
A Babylonian astronomer who lived in the third century BC.

Beth Eden:
(Hebrew) House of pleasure.

Bulla:
(Roman) An Amulet, a protective pouch worn around the neck like a locket. For boys, nine days to sixteen years of age. A pouch placed around the neck by one's mother as protection against evil spirits.

Casting lots:
A method to determine the will of the gods and a game of chance. Lots could be stakes with markings on them or stones with symbols and so forth. They would be dropped or thrown into a small area and then the results were interpreted by their arrangement or the symbols shown.

Centurion:
A Roman legion first sergeant or first lieutenant of a cohort (Depending on the source of information).

Chief Sabbath (Hebrew):
The Passover was observed during the month of Nisan (March/April). On the Sabbath Day of Passover the offering of first fruits of the harvest was made. Seven weeks later was the feast of Pentecost. The Sabbath in between first fruits and Pentecost are numbered as chief Sabbath.

Chuppah:
(Hebrew) The wedding canopy.

Commons:
A community backyard shared by all who border on it.

Council of Ruling Elders (Pharisees):

I can find no record of any such council. It is a figment of my imagination. But I am satisfied that some ruling body of some kind did exist and function as the council.

Despot:

From the Greek *despotes*, a lord, master, ruler with absolute power. A tyrannical ruler. An egotist or bully.

Cubit:

A measurement of about eighteen inches long.

Eileithyia:

The Greek goddess of childbirth.

Elders in Sepphoris:

The Pharisee ruling council of Galilee. I can find no record of any such council. It is a figment of my imagination. But I am satisfied that some ruling body of some kind did exist and function as the council.

Essenes:

(Hebrew) A small group that rejected temple worship as corrupt and lived a communal monastic lifestyle at Qumram.

The Fourteen:

(Sadducees) a.k.a. Council of the Temple and Judicature of the Priests. The ruling council of the Sadducees made up of temple priests.

Gladius:

The Roman short sword.

Herodians:

A loose-knit political following in support of the government of the Herodian family and Roman rule.

Indentured servant:
A contracted servant. One who is bound into service for a specified term.

Iscariot:
Ish (man), Kerioth (from Kerioth). A man from a town in southern Judea.

Ketubah:
Marriage contract.

Kinsman redeemer:
(Hebrew): A male relative who had the privilege or the responsibility to act in behalf of a relative who was in trouble, danger, or in need.

Leprosy:
From the Greek *lepros*. Scaly, an infectious disfiguring inflammation of the skin, rendering its victim ceremonially unclean.

Levites:
(Hebrew) Members of the tribe of Levi who were priests to Israel. They are responsible for the temple and the sacrifices. They are religious and social leaders of the Jewish people.

Mediator:
A go-between between two or more signers of a contract written by the Mediator, at the request of one of the signers. There is no such office in the Bible.

Mikveh:
(Hebrew) A ritual bath, used for the purpose of immersion to regain ritual purity.

Mishnah:
(Hebrew) The Oral Law. A refining conversation amongst Rabbis that has no end in sight.

Nard or Spikenard:

A class of aromatic amber-colored oil that comes from a flowering plant of the Valerian family. It grows in the Himalayas of Nepal, China, and India.

Neeman:

(Hebrew) A person accepted by the Pharisees as being careful in the observance of all religious duties, paying of tithes, and such. It was proper for a Pharisee to enter into commerce with such.

Pharisees:

(Hebrew) A group of about 6,000 influential Jews. They adhered to a strict observation of both the Written Laws (Torah and Talmud), the Oral Laws (Mishnaii), and the traditions of the elders. Long-time political and religious rivals of the Sadducees.

Pharisee of Pharisees:

One from a multi-generations of Pharisees.

Publican:

A tax farmer, that is, a collector of public revenue.

Retinue:

Entourage, attendants, followers.

Sadducees:

(Hebrew): A relatively small elite group from the ruling class of temple priests. Rulers of the Sanhedrin. They only followed the Written Law (Torah) and rejected the Written (Talmud), the Oral Laws (Mishnaii), and the traditions of the elders.

Sanhedrin:

The Israelite governing body and court systems.

Scribes:
Men specially trained in writing. They were influential as teachers and interpreters of the Written Law (Torah). A lawyer.

Sepphoris:
The one-time capital city of Galilee. It is about three and a half miles north of Nazareth.
The forerunner to Tiberius.

Sponge on a stick:
Public bathhouse attendance sold them to be used as toilet paper.

Sons of the bride chamber:
Friends or companions of the bridegroom. Members of the bridal procession that remain for the wedding feast.

Swaddled:
(Hebrew) Changing a diaper.

Tallit gadol:
(Hebrew) Prayer shawl.

Talmud:
The Babylonian Talmud, The Written Law, came about during the Babylonian captivity.

Tefillin:
(Hebrew) The phylacteries. Small wooden cases containing scripture. One is tied around the arm at the bicep with leather straps that extend down the arm to the hand. The other is tied to the forehead, with leather straps that hang down over the shoulder.

Tesserae:
(Roman) A type of dice game.

"These are my wishes":
Legal term required to identify a legal bequeath.

Thousand, thousand:
A number followed by six zeros, or a million or more. There is no number above "thousand" in either the Hebrew or Roman counting system.

Torah:
First five books of the Hebrew Bible.

Wine, cut four to one:
Wine, in the New Testament, is not wine; it is unfermented grape juice. "Cut four to one" is four parts of water to one part of wine. Honey is added to sweeten to taste.

Zealots:
One of several revolutionary groups who opposed the Roman occupation and rule over Israel.

THE SCROLL OF SCROLLS

Chapter 5

Baptist I, written by Judas Ben-Hakkatan of Jericho,
Matthew 3:5–10 and Luke 3:7–14 (22)
The Offspring of Vipers

Chapter 8

Baptist II, written by Abiathar Ben-Zadok of Jericho.
John 1:19–36 (26)
Voice Crying in the Wilderness

Chapter 9

Ben-Lahad I, written by Jada Ben-Lahad, the jeweler
John 2:14–16
A House of Merchandise

Ben-Gorion I, written by Jonathan Ben-Gorion
John 2:16–20
Destroy This Temple

Chapter 10

Levi I, written by the mediator Levi, with the withered hand
John 3:1–31 (32)
You Must Be Born Again

Chapter 12

Baptist III, written by Judas Ben-Hakkatan of Jericho
John 3:25–36 (33)
The Question from John's Disciples

Bar-Jathan I, written by Ahikar Bar-Jathan from Cana of Galilee
John 20:1–11
Wedding at Cana

Chapter 13

Galilean I, written by Judah Bar-Ohel of Nazareth.
Isaiah 61:1–2a and Luke 4:16–30 (39)
Today This Scripture Has Been Fulfilled in Your Ears

Galilean II, written by Ahikar Bar-Jathan, from Cana
John 4:46–50 (38)
The Nobleman's Son

Chapter 14

Galilean III, written by Chelub Bar-Abihail of Capernaum, tribe of Levi
Luke 4:31–36 and Luke 5:17–25 (42–46)
Unclean Spirit and Down from the Rooftop

Chapter 15

Galilean IV, written by Simon Bar-Gaal of Capernaum
Matthew 9:9–13, Mark 2:13–17, and Luke 5:27–32 (47)
A Tax Collector Named Levi.

Chapter 17

Galilean V, written by Chelub Bar-Abihail of Capernaum, tribe of Levi
Luke 5:29–38 (47)
Feasting and Fasting

Chapter 18

Galilean VI, written by Ahikar Bar-Jathan of Cana
Matthew 8:2–4 (45)
Healing the Leper

Chapter 19

Galilean VII, written by Simon Bar-Gaal of Capernaum
Matthew 12:1–8, Mark 2:23–28, and Luke 6:1–5 (50)
Ears of Corn

Galilean VIII, written by Simon Bar-Gaal of Capernaum
Matthew 12:9–14, Mark 3:1–6, and Luke 6:6–11 (51)
Man with a Withered Hand

Chapter 20

Galilean IX, written by Chelub Bar-Abihail of Capernaum of the tribe of Levi
Luke 7:2–10 (55)
Centurion's Servant in Capernaum

Chapter 22

Galilean X, written by Joseph Bar-Lecah, from the city of Nain
Luke 7:12–16 (56)
The Widow's Son, Raised from the Dead

Chapter 23

Galilean XI, written by Simon Bar-Gaal of Capernaum.
Luke 7:36–39 (59)
Anointed by a Sinner

Chapter 24

Galilean XII, written by Dodai Bar-Azariah
Luke 7:36–50 (59)
The Rest of the Story

Chapter 25

Galilean XIII, written by Beri Bar-Beracah of Arbela
Matthew 12:22–32 (61)
Beelzebub

Chapter 26

Galilean XIV, written by Chelub Bar-Abihail of Capernaum
Mark 5:22–43 and Luke 8:40–56 (67)
"Jairus' Daughter" and "The woman with a bloody issue."

Chapter 28

Galilean XV, written by Michael Bar-Carmi of Capernaum
Matthew 9:27–30a (68)
Two Blind Men

Chapter 30

Levi II, written by the mediator Levi
Matthew 14:1–11 (71)
Herod the Tetrarch

Chapter 32

Nathanael I, written by Nathanael Bar-Tholomew
Matthew 15:1–11 (77)
Hypocrites

Chapter 33

Nathanael II, written by Nathanael Bar-Tholomew
Luke 9:37–43 (87)
The Demonic Son

Chapter 34

Paulus I, written by Saul Ben-Paulus
John 7:14–24 (98)
My Teachings Are Not Mine

Council I, written by Levi as dictated by Shimon Ben-Gamaliel
John 7:25–36 and John 7:40–52 (96)
I Know Him

Chapter 35

Eglah I, written by Levi
John 8:2–11 (97)
She Was Not Condemned

Chapter 36

Chilion I, written by Levi
John 9:2–7 (100)
Now I Can See

Chapter 38

Chilion II, written by Levi
John 9:8–34 (100)
They Threw Him Out

Chapter 39

Ben-Benaiah III, written by Awnee Ben-Adon
John 9:35–41 (100)
Do You Believe?

Chapter 41

Nathanael III, written by Nathanael Bar-Tholomew
Luke 10:1–11
The Seventy

Chapter 42

Galilean XVI, written by Joseph Bar-Lecah
Luke 10:25–37 (103)
The Good Samaritan

Chapter 43

Bar-Lecah I, written by Joseph Bar-Lecah, from the city of Nain
Luke 13:10–17 (110)
18 Years

Paulus II, written by Saul Ben-Paulus
John 10:23–33 (111)
Tell Us Publicly

Chapter 44

Bethany I, written by the widow Athaliah, wife of Simon Ben-Judah
John 11:20–46 (118)
Lazarus

Council II
John 11:47–50
One Man Dies for the People

Chapter 45

Hakkatan I, written by Judas Ben-Hakkatan from Jericho
Mark 11:8–11 and John 12:12–14
Triumphal Entry

Nicodemus I
Mark 11:15–18
A Den of Robbers

Chapter 46

Hakkatan II
Luke 19:1–10
Zaccheus

Ben-Rawkal I
Mark 10:46–52
Blind Bar-Timeus

Chapter 47

Nicodemus II
Matthew 21:23–27
From Heaven or from Man?

Levi III
John 12:1–11
Anointed by Mary

Chapter 48

Levi VI
Mark 14:3–9
Anointed by a Woman

Paulus III
Matthew 22:34–40
Resurrection and Commandments

Chapter 49

Daniel I
John 18:2–23
Matthew 26:59–66

Matthew 27:11–26
John 14:2–3
Was It Legal?

Chapter 50

Daniel II
Jonah 2:1–11
Psalms 21, 22, 23

Chapter 52

Nicholaus I
John 19:32, Mark 43–46
Broken Legs and Burial

Eglah II
Mark 15:43–46
He Was Raised

Ben-Cleopas I
Luke 24:13–33
Our Hearts Were Burning

Chapter 53

Malchus I
Mark 14:43–50 and Matthew 28:11–15
Arrest and Bribe

Levi III
Matthew 28:16–20, Acts 1:4–13
Taken Up

THE SCROLL OF CHARACTERS

Chapter 1: The Retreat

(Indicates the meaning of names)

Jonathan Ben Gorion a.k.a. Nicodemus (True Name)
Shimon Ben Gamaliel (True Name)
Berossus, Babylonian Historian and Astrologer (True Name)
Rhodocus Ben-Merari "The Despot" and his followers (Traitorous son of Bitter)
Mediator Awnee Ben Adon, a.k.a. Nicholaus (Lowly son of the Master)

Chapter 2: Gabbai

Abishag, mistress of the third-floor ladies (King David's body warmer)
Lady, the street dog and companion of Nicholaus (The Planck family dog)
Jada Ben-Lahad, the Jeweler (God has cared, son of the tribe of Judah)
Mediator Levi, with a withered hand, the writer of the interview (son of the tribe of Levi)
Eglah, the third-floor chore girl (one of King David's eight wives)
Gabbai, servant of Judas of Jericho (Gatherer)

Chapter 3: The Romans

Centurion Marcus Gaius Manlius, of the Italian Band, Tenth Roman Legion (True Name)
Bar-Merari, the oil merchant (Fictitious)

Centurion Cornelius from Galilee (Fictitious)
King Herod the Tetrarch of Galilee (True Name)
Herodias, King Herod's wife (True Name)

Chapter 4: My Wishes

Pontius Pilatus, a prefect of Judah, an equestrian of the Pontii family. (True Name)
Mary Bat-Ruth, the wife of Sheva Ben Benaiah of the tribe of Judah. (fictitious)
Joann Bat-Ruth, the wife of Hantili the Hittite (fictitious)

Chapter 5: The Offspring of Vipers

Judas Ben-Hakkatan the writer of Baptist I and III (son of the little one)
John the Baptist a.k.a. The Baptist (True Name)
Zacchaeus, the chief of publicans in Jericho (True Name)

Chapter 6: The Mikvah

Abner Ben-Hilkiah, the council secretary (God's portion)
Chapter 7: Home

Chilion, blind son of Sheva Ben-Benaiah and Mary (Fictitious)
Bar-Shual a.k.a. the Fox of Galilee. Chore boy for the temple priests. (Son of a jackal or a fox)

Chapter 8: The Sandal Man

Abiathar Ben Zadok of Jericho, a writer of Baptist II (father of excellence son of the tribe of Aaron)
Abishag and Rizpah, servants of Abiathar Ben Zadok (King David's body warmers)
The sandal man (Fictitious)

Chapter 9: I Saw Him

Baruch Bar-Azariah from Galilee (Blessed son of whom God aids)
Dodai Bar-Azariah, the eldest son of Baruch (Loving son of whom God aids)

Chapter 11: Gods, Gods, and More Gods

Daniel Bar-Ananiel, mediator of the tribe of Naphtali (Prophet, Gracious)

Chapter 13: A Ring

Haggith, the daughter of Caiaphas (King David's fifth wife)
Malchus, the servant of Caiaphas (True Name)
Sarah, the maiden servant of Haggith (the wife of Abraham)
Caiaphas, the high priest (True Name)
Judah Ben Ohel of Nazareth, writer of Galilean I (son of a tenant)
Ahikar Bar-Jathan, from Cana of Galilee, writer of Galilean II (precious brother, descendant of a prophet)

Chapter 14: Contracts

Hakkatan, a Levite and servant of Abner Ben-Hilkiah. (The little one)
Chelub Bar-Abihail, of the tribe of Levi, writer of Galilean III, V, IX, and XIV (basket, son of father of strength)
Hamutal, second-floor servant girl.

Chapter 15: The Tax Collector

Tawah Bar-Gaal of Capernaum, writer of Galilean III (To cheat, deceive, misuse. The son of contempt)
Merab, the head cook and manager of the second-floor kitchen. (King Saul's daughter, David's first wife)

Chapter 18: Touched a Leper

Baara, Eglah's helper. (One of the wives of Shaharaim)
Cozbi, Eglah's helper. (A Midianitish woman)
Nathanael Bar-Tholomew, one of the Twelve Disciples (True Name)
Simon Ben-Cleopas, the indentured servant of Simon Bar-Gaal. One of the two men on the road to Emmaus. (True Name)

Chapter 19: More Bother than He Is Worth

Ben-Resheph, a Pharisee and a friend of Shimon Ben Hithpael. (Son of Fire)

Chapter 20: It's a Girl

Zilpah, one of the ladies of the commons and Eglah's best friend
Huldah, Eglah's daughter (The prophetess and keeper of the royal wardrobe)
Eileithyia, the Greek goddess of childbirth

Chapter 21: The Question

Reaiah, Azariah's youngest son (seen by God)
Naam, Azariah's middle son (Pleasant)

Chapter 22: The Widow's Son

Joseph Bar-Lecah of the city of Nain, writer of Galilean X (Of the tribe of Judah)

Chapter 23: Anointed by a Sinner

Jabin Ben-Geber his first secretary to Caiaphas (He understands, son of man)
Scribe Judah Ben-Paruah (Gloomy)

Pharisee Tobiel Ben-Shobai (God is good, son of captive)
Mediator Joseph Ben-Uzziah (God is my strength)

Chapter 24: The Rest of the Story

James the carpenter, the brother of Jesus (True Name)
Mary the mother of Jesus (True Name)
Simon the brother of Jesus (True Name)
Jonathon Ben-Jadon (He will judge)

Chapter 25: Beelzebub

Towb Ben-Rawkal, a good friend of Nicholaus (Good merchant)
Beri Bar-Beracah, a Pharisee of the tribe of Asher, writer of Galilean
XIII. (Mighty warrior, son of blessing)

Chapter 26: Jairus's Daughter

Jairus, ruler of the synagogue in Capernaum. (True Name)

Chapter 27: The Testimonies Begin

Widow Ben-Shobai (Captivity)

Chapter 28: Imprint of a Signet

Michael Bar-Carmi and a Pharisee of Pharisees of Capernaum, writer
of Galilean XV. (Who is like God, son of vinedresser)
Pekah, the Eunuch, servant of King Herod the Tetrarch of Galilee
(Opened eyed)

Chapter 33: Down from the Mountain

Bar-Abbas, a.k.a. Barabbas
Bar-Achan, the Zealot (son of a troublemaker, fictitious)

Bar-Dimeus, a Zealot (Fictitious)
Bar-Gestas, a Zealot (Fictitious)

Chapter 34: My Teachings Are Not Mine

Saul Ben-Paulus of Tarsus (son of a little man)

Chapter 35: She Was Not Condemned

Rizpah, a servant girl.

Chapter 41: The Seventy

Judah Ben-Penuel, a courier from the High Council in Sepphoris

Chapter 44: Lazarus

Athaliah, the widow of Simon Ben-Judah, who was a member of the Council of Ruling Elders
Mary and Martha, sisters living in Bethany (True Names)
Lazarus, the brother of Mary and Martha, friend of Jesus (True Name)

Chapter 47: Mary's Anointing

Judas Iscariot, one of the Disciples of Jesus (True Name)

Chapter 48: Anointed by a Woman

Simon the Leper (True Name)

Chapter 49: Was It Legal?

Annas. Father-in-law of Caiaphas (True Name)

Chapter 52: It Was Empty

Mary Magdalene
Joanna
Mary the mother of James. At tomb of Jesus for his burial anointing.

THE ASTRONOMY SCROLL

To see the events described, you must first have access to a planetarium or a computer with good astronomy software. You are going to want to see what was recorded in Rome.

Rome I: Date: March 23, -7. Time: 6:59 a.m. Location: Latitude 41 deg. 54 min. 10 sec. north by longitude 12 deg. 29 min. 47 sec. East. Facing east.

Rome II: Date: March 12, -6. Time: 7:14 p.m. Location: Latitude 41 deg. 54 min. 10 sec. north by longitude 12 deg. 29 min. 47 sec. East. Facing west.

Alexandria I: Date: March 23, -7. Time: 5:39 a.m. Location: Latitude 30 deg. 12 min. 00 sec north by longitude 29 deg. 55 min. 7 sec. East. Facing east.

Alexandria II: Date: March 12, -6. Time: 6:15 p.m. Location: Latitude 30 deg. 12 min. 00 sec north by longitude 29 deg. 55 min. 7 sec. East. Facing west.

There will be a number of possibilities presented as to the significance of this event, and I will not confirm or deny my acceptance of any of them as true.

Happy investigating.

ABOUT THE AUTHOR

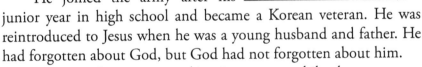

Rev. William E. Planck was first confronted with the question, "What then should I do with Jesus called Christ?" When it was put to him by an evangelist in the local neighborhood park, sitting at a picnic table. He was four years old.

He was shipped off to military school when he was ten years old. He spent his teen years skipping school and working in his family's taverns.

He joined the army after his junior year in high school and became a Korean veteran. He was reintroduced to Jesus when he was a young husband and father. He had forgotten about God, but God had not forgotten about him.

He spent thirty years working in an automobile plant as a security officer, firefighter, and industrial EMT.

After retirement, he was called to attend Bible college. Upon graduation, he was ordained an elder in the Church of the Nazarene.

He and Mary, his wife of fifty-seven years, now live on the Indian Lake Nazarene campground near Vicksburg, Michigan.

They have two children, six grandchildren, and eight great-grandchildren.

The Ben-Adon Scrolls is Rev Planck's first novel.